"So You Want to Play Rough, Do You?"

Lance wrenched Jill against his body, and they both tumbled backward into the water.

He maintained his vise grip on her slender shoulders, unwittingly pulling her below the surface before she was able to gulp in a fresh breath of air.

Weak and exhausted when they resurfaced, Jill sagged against him. A hand tipped her chin upward, as Lance scrutinized her face. "Are you all right?"

Still too shaken to speak, Jill shook her head, her luminous eyes gazing into his in confusion. Had she mistakenly heard concern in his deep voice? As she watched, those compelling lips descended, covering hers with a kiss that drew her into a whirlpool of feeling, drowning her in a tidal wave of desire. . . .

ELIZABETH REYNOLDS
resides in Poughkeepsie, New York. This is her first Silhouette Romance.

Dear Reader:

During the last year, many of you have written to Silhouette telling us what you like best about Silhouette Romances and, more recently, about Silhouette Special Editions. You've also told us what else you'd like to read from Silhouette. With your comments and suggestions in mind, we've developed SILHOUETTE DESIRE.

SILHOUETTE DESIREs will be on sale this June, and each month we'll bring you four new DESIREs written by some of your favorite authors—Stephanie James, Diana Palmer, Rita Clay, Suzanne Simms and many more.

SILHOUETTE DESIREs may not be for everyone, but they are for those readers who want a more sensual, provocative romance. The heroines are slightly older—women who are actively involved in their careers and the world around them. If you want to experience all the excitement, passion and joy of falling in love, then SILHOUETTE DESIRE is for you.

I'd appreciate any thoughts you'd like to share with us on new SILHOUETTE DESIRE, and I invite you to write to us at the address below:

Karen Solem
Editor-in-Chief
Silhouette Books
P.O. Box 769
New York, N.Y. 10019

ELIZABETH REYNOLDS
An Ocean of Love

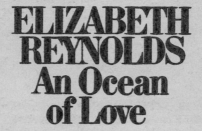

Silhouette Romance

Published by Silhouette Books New York

America's Publisher of Contemporary Romance

SILHOUETTE BOOKS, a Simon & Schuster Division of
GULF & WESTERN CORPORATION
1230 Avenue of the Americas, New York, N.Y. 10020

Distributed by Pocket Books

ISBN: 0-671-57158-3

First Silhouette Books printing June, 1982

10 9 8 7 6 5 4 3 2 1

Map by Tony Ferrara

America's Publisher of Contemporary Romance

Printed in the U.S.A.

An Ocean of Love

Chapter One

Jill felt the threads of self-control beginning to snap, one by one. For weeks she'd had to stand by impotently watching her stepmother die, slowly, agonizingly. Now she had to battle back the urge to cry out hysterically, and attempt to maintain the facade, at least, of total control. But she felt her hands clutch convulsively at the arms of her chair as she faced Mr. Formby, the family lawyer, across his desk.

"You mean my stepmother never made out a will? And Daddy hadn't made provisions in his in the event of her death?"

Her low, soft voice threatened to crack. Ice-blue eyes stared incredulously out of a delicately molded face.

Mr. Formby's glance roamed compassionately over the pretty dark-haired girl sitting opposite him a moment, before resignedly adjusting his black-framed glasses and admitting, "Yes, Jill, I'm afraid that's exactly it." He sighed heavily, raising his hands in a helpless gesture. "I did try repeatedly to get Lucy to rectify the situation, but you know how irresponsible and selfish she was." He made the accusation knowing full well that the girl before him would exhibit her unfailing loyalty to what little family she had had, and defend her stepmother. He wasn't disappointed.

"Oh, now, Mr. Formby, you know after Daddy's death she fell apart. She was always the type that needed a man to take care of her. It was just her nature. She could never pick up the pieces after that."

Mr. Formby raised his hands in surrender.

"All right, young lady. But how you can still see Lucy Taggert kindly after all she put you through in the last few years, and especially in the last six months, is beyond me." He drew some papers from a folder on his desk with an uncomfortable expression on his face. "Unfortunately, your loyalty, however misplaced, is going to be unrewarded. Even if Lucy had left anything to you, it would all have to be sold to settle the debts against your father's estate."

Jill's eyes became even bigger as she straightened in her leather-upholstered chair. "What do you mean, debts against Daddy's estate?"

Mr. Formby's face took on a haggard look.

"I wish I could somehow shield you from all this," he sighed. "But there were—uh—debts incurred by your father while he was alive which your stepmother failed to clear up. And from the time of his death until her own, Lucy added to them. I was appointed executor of his estate, so I was the one who dealt with the bills and tradespeople."

Jill sank back in her chair in a posture of defeat. "So that's why there were never any bills around," she murmured. "I asked Lucy about it once in one of her more sober moments, and she insisted she was taking care of them. She said all I had to do was make sure there were adequate supplies and food in the house. She always seemed to have money for those."

Jill remembered all the times Lucy had tossed a wad of bills, usually fifties, at her, and they had miraculously kept the larder filled. Then a horrifying thought struck her and she raised suspicious eyes to the lawyer.

"Where did she get all that money from for keeping up the house and to support her . . ."—Jill's tongue stumbled at having to say the next word, but she managed to force it out—". . . drinking?"

Mr. Formby coughed nervously and answered, "Well, I know that she received a minimal sum from the estate to pay for the essentials, but you couldn't have eaten exactly like queens." In spite of his age, he looked flushed and embarrassed. "She may have received money from her—er—friends," he suggested delicately.

"You mean she took money from her innumerable boyfriends?" Jill stated baldly. At Mr. Formby's shocked expression, she added, "Oh, Mr. Formby, I'm twenty-two going on forty-three. I saw what Lucy was like. I saw all those ever-changing men who brought her home after the bars had closed at one in the morning. They were always so drunk they didn't know I was there. And if they had, I don't think they would have cared." Jill stopped, realizing that she was beginning to sound sorry for herself, and she didn't want Mr. Formby's sympathy. What she wanted was something she hadn't had since her mother had died ten years previously: security. And with the death of a stepmother who had been a source of trouble rather than security, it looked like she wasn't any closer to receiving it, what with debts against the depleted estate of her father.

The lawyer was shaking his head slowly and looking at Jill with amazement. "It's a wonder you've turned out to be the normal, nicely mannered young lady you are," he marveled. Then he cleared his throat and abruptly got down to business. "Well, the first thing you will have to do is to go through Lucy's things. Though anything of value will naturally have to be sold, if you find anything of purely sentimental value, make a note of it and we'll see that you get it after the auction."

"Is that how you're going to get rid of the house, too?" Something in Jill's voice communicated her worry about the future.

Mr. Formby removed his glasses and ran a weary hand through his gray hair. "Yes, I'm afraid so, my dear." He paused, reluctant to ask the next question. "Have you thought about what you're going to do? I know taking care of Lucy and the house kept you from continuing your education and, well . . ." He ended helplessly, concern etching myriad lines in his brow.

Jill sighed deeply, her gentle mouth drooping. "Well, no. I . . . I really haven't given it much thought, what with the funeral and everything. I . . . I suppose I'll have to move out of the house?" she asked dejectedly.

Mr. Formby nodded unhappily. It was one of fate's cruel tricks, he was thinking, for a girl so young and undeserving to have her whole world crumble down around her within the span of five days.

They had buried her last known relative yesterday, when Lucy had been lowered into the cold, forbidding ground. But, for Jill the future looked equally cold and forbidding. Without the benefit of college, she was untrained for any worthwhile position. It looked like she was condemned to an immediate future, at least, of waitressing or motel cleaning.

Jill looked up to see Mr. Formby's kindly face regarding her with concern, and she decided she had better stop wallowing in self-pity. Squaring her shoulders, she rose, extending a hand to the lawyer.

As he took the proffered hand in his and held it firmly, he begged, "Please don't hate me for having to play the heavy, my dear. If I could have spared you all this, I would have moved mountains, if possible, to do so."

Jill squeezed the smooth old hand affectionately. Heartfelt emotion accented her voice as she assured him she didn't. "Of course not, Mr. Formby. You have to do your job. Just like a surgeon sometimes has to perform an amputation, it isn't pleasant, but it's necessary."

The elderly lawyer flinched at her choice of analogy even as he acknowledged that it was appropriate. He did feel that by doing his job he was disabling a young, vibrant girl, with everything to look forward to, for life.

"Please, if I can help you in any way at all, don't hesitate to call."

Jill nodded, then turned away before he could see how deeply his solicitude affected her. It was unfortunate that Lucy hadn't felt the same way, instead of resenting the anchor a young girl of seventeen had been to her. But dwelling on what might have been did no good, and Jill resolutely put all thoughts of Lucy on the shelf for the present and went home to the house that soon would no longer welcome her.

Winter was giving warning of its imminent arrival, with late November storm clouds amassed overhead. Along with the chill was a stiff breeze. Jill hunched her

11

shoulders as she let herself into the big two-story frame house, using the back door near the garage. She felt the weather was an apt accompaniment to her mood, and a melancholy feeling set in as she paused in the kitchen.

It was dinnertime, but she had no appetite. Instead of fixing something to eat, she wandered from room to room, lovingly touching all the furniture that had belonged to her parents. Anything that Lucy had purchased or had brought to her father's second marriage was carefully avoided. She stopped when she came to her stepmother's room, steeling herself for an unpleasant task. For the most part, Lucy had kept all of her personal possessions in her room, and Jill forced herself to approach the dresser, repelled at the thought of going through the dead woman's things.

The top two drawers of the polished oak dresser held many articles of lingerie, and Jill's inspection of the bottom two drawers revealed a number of sweaters. As she fingered the fine material of the woolens and mohairs, her eyes narrowed. It was strange how Lucy had had plenty of money for the surfeit of clothing she was always buying, when Mr. Formby had plainly stated that there had been only enough for the essentials. These sweaters weren't of the dime-store variety, and neither were the dresses, pantsuits, and shoes in the closet. Jill was forced to admit that for all her faults, Lucy had never been tight-fisted about stocking Jill's wardrobe, either. It was a puzzle, one for which Jill had no immediate answer. Surely all those boyfriends who had floated in and out of Lucy's life hadn't given her such a financial abundance.

She slowly closed the bottom dresser drawer, reflecting on the problem, then noticed that something was preventing the drawer from closing completely. She pulled it out and tried again, making sure the sides were aligned properly, but the maneuver seemed to aggravate the situation, instead. She pulled the entire drawer out, letting it down gently on the pile carpeting. Peering into the empty space, she spied what looked like a crumpled envelope wedged against the back. As she reached in and pulled the envelope out, she heard the tearing sound made as the tape that had been used to attach it to the inside of the back of the dresser released its hold.

The envelope was old-looking, and the tape had ripped off a piece of its worn surface, the part with the postmark, so it was now impossible to tell how old it was. It was strange that Lucy would go to so much trouble to hide a love letter, Jill reflected, when no one would ever have gone through her dresser when she was alive.

But curiosity was always a woman's tempter, and Jill couldn't resist peeking inside to see what Lucy had felt needed to be concealed so thoroughly. She drew out the bedraggled letter, obviously one that had been well read. Sitting on the floor before the open drawer, Jill checked to see who had been the sender of the mysterious letter. A look of incredulity came over her face.

As she read the name, a bittersweet memory transported her back to a time ten years before. It had been an awful time for the twelve-year-old girl with long brown-black braids and eyes the color of cornflowers. She had had dimples then, too, but only one person had seen them revealed by a rarely flashed smile. And that one person had come into Jill's troubled life at a time when she was experiencing grief that had never been equaled since.

Her beloved mother had died suddenly in the night, of a stroke. She could remember padding out into the hallway in her robe and slippers when unaccustomed

13

noise from voices she didn't recognize had awakened her. The hallway had seemed filled to bursting with strangers in white outfits, and at the far end of the hall she saw her father weeping profusely over an inert form on a low, rolling stretcher. She hadn't known who was on that stretcher, since a white sheet completely covered the body, but it was revealed to her in the harsh light of morning that her mother was gone.

She had been bustled back to her room and tucked in bed by a nervously clucking neighbor woman who refused to answer her questions. After the woman had left, Jill had risen and gone to her bedroom window, which overlooked the front of the house, to watch the men in white roll the still form out into the starless night, lift it into the back of an ambulance, and drive away without the accompaniment of a siren.

Sheer terror had kept the sensitive pre-teen in her room until the sun crept over her windowsill. Then, as stealthily as those early fingers of dawn, she had made her way down the hall to her mother's room. For some reason unknown to her, her parents had established separate sleeping quarters two years before.

When she had pushed the door slowly open after receiving no answer to her light tap, she had found her mother's bed empty—the sheets, blanket, and even the pillow had all been removed. Then the explanation for the previous night's happenings jolted through her brain in a searingly painful flash.

With an agonized cry, she had dashed out into the hall and had run with tears streaming down her pale cheeks to her father's room. Attempts to awaken him had proved futile. He had seemed to be unconscious, and as she had looked at him in horror, a stranger had walked into his room.

That had been Jill's first introduction to Lucy De-

Prey. She was a young divorcée who had moved into the house across the street, but Jill had never really noticed her before. Lucy had drawn her from the room, explaining that Gordon Taggert had been given a sedative. When it wore off, he would awaken.

The memories of that time were still so painful that Jill now found to her discomfort that she was crying. Huge tears were rolling down, leaving salty tracks on her cheeks. She gave in and allowed the first tears of self-pity to rack her slender body in a strangely cathartic fashion.

When at last she had wept her fill, she gazed at the bold handwriting on the letter lying on her lap. It belonged to the one person that had found time to comfort a frightened young girl in the chaotic days that had followed her mother's death. Jill looked at the signature, affixed with boldly crossed T's, and a faint smile threatened to bring out the dimples in her salty cheeks. Matthew Lane had been her mother's only living relative, and had come all the way from his home on the Florida coast to attend her funeral in the midwestern town of Topeka, Kansas. It had been the first time Jill had ever heard of him. And the last.

She remembered how, amid all the hustle and bustle of neighbors and friends calling or dropping by, Uncle Matt, as he had instructed her to call him, had sought her out, seeing if she was all right, taking her for walks down quiet tree-lined streets, and teaching her how to play chess on the antique chessboard that was her father's pride and joy. Somehow her father had never had the time to teach his only child the intricacies of the ancient game of symbolic war, but Uncle Matt had. And she had loved it, even though he always won. She remembered that one of the faceless people who seemed to flow in and out of the house those days had

asked, "Why don't you let the poor child win sometimes, Matthew? You're going to make her frustrated."

Matthew Lane had looked at Jill with a brooding
intensity before replying. His answer had hinted at the
trouble he had seen ahead for her with his advanced
age that she as a child had never suspected.

"Because she's going to have to learn to fight for
every good thing she wants," he had said quietly. "And
to let her win would be morally wrong. She's got the
stuff. Mark my word." Then he had leaned forward and
winked at her, reaching out to playfully tug one of her
braids. "And I'll bet you're going to make a terrific
chess player, huh, Jilly Dilly?"

Dawning maturity had made Jill embarrassed by the
nickname he had given her, even as she warmed to the
obvious affection in his gravelly voice.

When the funeral was all over, Matthew Lane had
disappeared from Jill's life. And Lucy DePrey had
come to stay. Within six months she was the new Mrs.
Gordon Taggert, and a new era had been ushered in at
the Taggert home.

Jill winced mentally and firmly closed the door on
further painful remembrances. She had read only the
salutation and the signature, wanting to establish in her
mind which of Lucy's many discarded lovers had written. Now she began reading the words, which were
dated a few months after her father's death, five years
before.

Her delicate jaw dropped open in disbelief. It was
preposterous! How could Lucy have done it? She read
furiously, her eyes practically flying over the words in
her haste. It was horrible! Her stepmother had written
to Matt Lane requesting an outrageous sum of money.
Apparently the request had been in answer to an earlier
letter from Matt, who had offered her money to settle

the debts her father had left. There had been a check for ten thousand dollars promised, but Jill knew the money had never been used to pay off any debts. It was obvious that that money had been the source of all the expensive clothes, the good meals, the endless supply of liquor Lucy had imbibed for the past five years, and whatever else she had spent it on.

Jill uttered a sound of disgust as she rose unsteadily to her feet. As she flexed her cramped muscles, she reread the last sentence of the letter: "If there is ever anything else I can do for you, please don't hesitate to call on me."

She raised her head, staring in front of her. Could this be the answer to her dilemma? Could it have been the hand of fate that had caused her to pull out that drawer of Lucy's and discover the letter?

Almost fearfully, Jill went out to the kitchen. Could she contact Uncle Matt after all these years? He had been old then; by now he must surely be in his seventies. And the address on the envelope—did he still live there? Would he even remember her? Ten years was a long time.

She made herself a cup of strong black coffee, hoping the stimulant would aid her in making a decision. She went, almost as if in a dreamlike trance, out to the living room, across the hall, and into the study. Shakily, she put the cup of steaming liquid down on the desk, then removed the cover of the typewriter. Then, changing her mind, she replaced it, choosing instead some pale pink stationery of Lucy's. She began to write.

Chapter Two

The 707 taxied to a smooth stop and the passengers began collecting their hand luggage and removing coats and jackets from the overhead storage bins. Suppressing a rising sense of excitement, Jill forced herself to calmly gather her handbag and light raincoat. Following her disembarking fellow passengers, she arrived in the relatively small reception area, her eyes sweeping over the crowd that was waiting to greet the travelers.

Her uncle had sent word that his secretary would be meeting Jill's plane, apologizing for his inability to do it himself. He hadn't explained his reasons, and Jill had worked valiantly to keep herself from feeling disappointed. After all, he was quite elderly, and for all she knew, he might be confined to a bed or a wheelchair.

Jill studied the crowd, many of whom were now escorting friends or relatives away, for a woman, perhaps middle-aged, who could be the promised secretary. So convinced was she that a woman was going to meet her, that when a man stepped out from the crowd and spoke her name, almost inaudibly, she stared at him, her obvious confusion registering on her expressive face.

He stood well over six feet tall, which gave him an advantage of quite a few inches over Jill's five-foot-seven height. Jill absently decided he was about thirty-three years old. He had broad muscular shoulders, clothed in a tight-fitting knit shirt, tapering to narrow hips above muscled thighs, and his stance as he returned her scrutiny was definitely aggressive. His face seemed chiseled from stone, with high cheekbones and a well-shaped mouth, with a sensually full lower lip. Hard steel-gray eyes narrowed above a straight nose, assessing her as thoroughly as she was abstractly examining him.

"Miss Taggert?" he repeated. Jill nodded. He held out his hand, and she took it in still-apparent bewilderment. "I'm Lance Darrel, Mr. Lane's second-in-command. I'm here to escort you to his home," the man informed her with an economy of words.

"Oh." Jill gulped, still not certain if the man had genuinely been sent by her Uncle Matt. She shook the extended hand with characteristic firmness. "I'm pleased to meet you. You said you're Mr. Lane's second-in-command? But I thought . . ."

"Yes. Mrs. Flemming was supposed to be here, but Mr. Lane thought it was more appropriate for me to come, instead." Lance Darrel's words were laced with scarcely veiled sarcasm, which puzzled Jill.

"Oh, well, I don't think—" she began, only to be rudely interrupted by Lance.

"No, I don't suppose you do." This time there was

no mistaking the faint tinge of disapproval. Lance Darrel obviously felt that his time was better spent elsewhere. Jill tried not to bridle at his tone of voice.

He indicated she should follow him and led her to the baggage-claim area. Jill quickly identified her two new suitcases, which she had bought rather like a symbolic gesture prior to making this trip to Florida, and with the bags clamped in Lance's grip, he led her out to the street.

Although it was early January, the weather was fair, with the temperature in the low sixties. The sky overhead was startlingly blue, and Jill reveled in her escape from winter as she followed Lance to the parking lot. A late-model Mercedes glistened in the afternoon sun, and it was with a sense of dismay that Jill found herself being led to it. She wondered if the car was Lance's or her uncle's. Either way, it meant money.

Lance caught the wide-eyed look with which she was regarding the car, and his brow darkened. He threw her two bags in the trunk as if they were sacks of potatoes and slammed the lid shut.

"If you don't mind, I'd appreciate your according my cases a little more respect," Jill informed him icily.

"Certainly, Miss Taggert!" Lance's cold eyes slashed to her momentarily before ricocheting away, smoldering in resentment.

Something in the region of Jill's stomach tightened convulsively. What was the matter with this insufferable man? What could she have possibly done to elicit this much hostility?

When Lance opened the door to the passenger's side, she slid in, trying not to flinch as he slammed the door with a violence that was totally unwarranted. She decided he'd gone far enough, and as soon as he got in behind the leather-encased steering wheel, she confronted him.

"All right, Mr. Darrel, what seems to be the problem? What in the world have I done?" Her blue eyes darkened to a color that those who knew her realized presaged storm clouds.

Lance Darrel turned in his seat to study her with infuriating slowness.

"You have come down here under the pretense of being Matthew Lane's grandniece," he drawled, his voice deliberately insulting, "when anyone knows that the daughter of Gordon Taggert died five years ago. You may have been able to fool the old man with that pitiful letter of yours, but not me. I know you for what you really are: a fraud; a gold digger. So if you think you can worm your way into his kindly old heart, perhaps with the idea that you can get some money out of 'Uncle Matt,' then be aware right from the start that I'm onto you, and I won't let you take an easily fooled old man to the financial cleaners."

Jill stared incredulously at him. Her breath seemed trapped in her chest. His words were unbelievable. A stifled gasp escaped her lips before she could think of a suitable reply.

"What do you mean, Gordon Taggert's daughter is supposed to be dead?" she finally managed to say.

Lance's eyes narrowed as he tersely answered, "She died in the same automobile crash that killed Gordon."

Jill allowed herself the luxury of taking offense at his manner. Summoning up her iciest tones, she stated, "Well, I can assure you that I *am* alive. And as for worming my way into his heart, let's see if Uncle Matt doesn't recognize me, and let him be the judge. Does that suit you?" Her blue eyes shot smoky sparks as she tilted her chin defiantly.

"No, that's not acceptable to me." The words, issued through clenched teeth, were bitter with regret. Lance followed by saying, "But it will have to do. However, let me tell you, Jill Taggert, or whoever you are, that you had better be the genuine article, or you'll regret the day you arrived." His eyes glinted cruelly, leaving Jill in no doubt that he was a man who would carry out his threats, no matter what he had to go through to do so.

Jill settled back in the seat, breathing hard from the exertion of this verbal confrontation. The last thing she had expected when she had disembarked from the airplane was this hostile welcome. When she saw her uncle, she was going to give him her opinion of his second-in-command.

She glanced surreptitiously at the man at her side whose lean, dark hands, no doubt tanned a shade of teak by the southern sun, were expertly guiding the car out onto the highway that fronted the Daytona airport. He had dark brown hair, growing low over the collar of his shirt. It rose in waves from a smooth forehead, as darkly tanned as his hands. His legs seemed out of place in the front of the car, even with its generous proportions. He looked like the type that would be more at home out-of-doors. Jill wondered what his job as second-in-command entailed. For that matter, she didn't know what her uncle needed with one, for she knew nothing about her uncle's occupation, if he had one.

The trip continued in silence, with Jill seething in her corner of the front seat, awaiting the moment that should have been joyful. She tried not to let the tears flow, although they burned the backs of her eyelids. The only way to deal with this man was to show that nothing he said could puncture the bubble of self-confidence she was firmly wrapping around herself. She knew in her heart that his ludicrous accusation was groundless, and as soon as she met Uncle Matt again, there would be adequate proof in her favor. Then she would sit back smugly and watch this too-sure-of-himself man eat humble pie. She felt sure that even after ten years her uncle would still be able to see a remnant of the awkward pre-teen he had visited.

Lance turned the car down a long drive lined with orange trees, and she caught a glimpse of the ocean beyond, its whitecaps creaming in to wash over the sand. They arrived at the end of the drive to halt before a large two-story house.

Jill let herself out of the car, uncaring whether Lance was going to play the chauvinist to the last detail and open the car door for her. As she stepped out, the main door to the white-painted house was thrown open by a tall, burly white-haired man who strode down the steps with the vigor of a young one.

"Jill! At last!" he cried, reaching the bottom step as she realized that this vibrant personality was her uncle. Here was no frail type needing confinement in a sickbed, nor one who would invoke the protective instincts of Lance Darrel. This man looked perfectly capable of caring for himself. In fact, he looked hardly different from the way she had remembered. It raised Jill's confidence several notches, and with heartfelt fervor she threw herself into his outstretched arms.

"Uncle Matt," she sobbed, returning his firm bear hug. "It's been ten long years, and yet I feel like it was only yesterday when you were teaching me how to play chess on our back porch."

"Do you play any better?" the older man asked, a wide grin splitting his lined face.

"You just try me and see if I don't beat you now. I've had plenty of time to practice," she teased back.

Her uncle laughed heartily, releasing her as far as holding her at arm's length, his big hands resting lightly on her shoulders.

"Let me get a good look at you, girl." His eyes made a thorough appraisal, one that didn't embarrass her as Lance's had. He chuckled in approval, his light blue eyes twinkling. "Well, you didn't grow much, but you sure redistributed what you had."

The remark, made in front of Lance's sardonic face, brought a pink tinge to Jill's cheeks.

"What did you expect after ten years?" She laughed, trying to appear unflustered before the aggressive set of the younger man's head. A quick glance at his face had relayed the information that, instead of reassuring him, this meeting of grandniece and uncle seemed to have angered him in some way. Perhaps he was worried that his undoubtedly close relationship with Matt was going to be crowded out by a new one with Jill. Well, she decided, it was too bad if Lance Darrel felt she was a threat to the cozy friendship between the two men. There was a tie between Matt and Jill, and she was here to cement it further after the ten-year separation.

Just then an elderly man shuffled out the front door. Matt broke off staring at Jill long enough to say, "John, please put Miss Taggert's things in the purple room," then turned back to regard her with another searching look.

John relieved Lance of the cases he had just removed from the Mercedes, and struggled up the steps with them, muttering under his breath all the way. Jill watched him in disbelief and turned to her uncle.

"Is he always that irritable?"

Matthew Lane broke out with a booming laugh.

24

"Always! But he's as much an old friend as a hired man, and we've been together for forty years." He relinquished his hold on her shoulders and threw an arm across them instead. "Come, my dear. Let's go have a drink to celebrate our reunion. Lance," he called over his shoulder, "as soon as you've put the car in the garage, come join us for a bottle of champagne." His voice rang out jubilantly, and Lance frowned.

"Champagne, Matt?" he asked, with one dark brow raised quizzically.

"Certainly, my boy. We have something to celebrate!" His eyes gentled on Jill a moment. "The return of my grandniece from the grave."

His announcement rooted Jill to the spot. Here was the second person within the hour to refer to her death. It was time to get some facts straight, and she stepped lightly out of her uncle's hold, pivoted to face him, and asked, "Uncle Matt, why did you and Mr. Darrel think I had died?" She spoke slowly, as an odd tightening began in her stomach.

There was a strange sense of foreboding hanging heavy in the air as Lance Darrel and Matthew Lane exchanged looks; then her uncle turned to her and laid his hands caressingly on her shoulders.

"Honey, I have to ask you a question. Okay?" His voice was kindly, but there was a burning sense of purpose in the depths of his blue eyes. Like Jill's, they had darkened slightly under some inner strain.

"Yes, Uncle Matt," Jill agreed curiously.

"What was the name I called you when I came for your mother's funeral?" His eyes now glowed with expectancy, but Jill failed to see how his nickname for her had anything to do with the subject under discussion.

"Why, you know, Uncle Matt." She glanced ner-

25

vously at Lance, standing there with an unreadable expression on his dark face. For some reason she couldn't yet identify, she was loath to say that name in his presence, but knew she had to answer her uncle's question.

"'Jilly Dilly,' Uncle Matt," she murmured, hoping Lance couldn't hear her feather-soft answer.

It was a futile wish, because Matt Lane whooped, grabbing Jill around the waist, and twirled her around.

"That's it! Jilly Dilly!" he shouted. He turned to Lance. "I told you Lucy was capable of lying. And as soon as this young lady got out of the car, I knew she was Jill."

He brought his happy gaze back to rest on Jill's startled face. "She has the same blue eyes she inherited from her mother's side of the family, and the same black hair as her father. And I'll never forget those dimples." He reached out to stroke her cheek, but Jill's mind had latched onto something he'd said, and she had to have it clarified.

"Uncle Matt, what do you mean you thought Lucy could have lied?"

Matt Lane's face sagged.

"I hate to call the dead names, but Lucy Taggert was a liar, among other things. She said you died that night your father did. She wrote and told me you were both in the car at the time." He cast his eyes to the ground beneath his feet, and wearily went on. "She said she had been all but wiped out financially burying you two, so I offered her money."

Jill nodded, remembering the letter. "And she had the audacity to ask for ten thousand dollars," she said heavily.

"Yes, but how did you know that?"

Jill explained about finding the letter and how she

26

had gotten up her courage to write, not knowing if her uncle would remember her or even if he still lived at the same address. She hadn't revealed that information in her letter to him; instead, she'd simply mentioned her stepmother's death, the need for the sale of the house and contents, and her being at loose ends.

Her uncle's return letter had come within a week, inviting her to fly down to his home outside Daytona Beach. Enclosed with the letter had been a generous check to cover her air fare and any other expenses she might have, but she had sent the check back, preferring to provide for her own needs. Her unscrupulous stepmother had taken more than she deserved from her uncle, and Jill had no desire to add insult to injury.

Within a month she had finished the inventory on the house, and, leaving a list of the very few items she had wanted for herself with the lawyer, she had boarded the jet that brought her cast.

Now, within two hours of her arrival, she was uncovering more of the pieces to the awful puzzle her stepmother had left as a disgraceful legacy.

Something of her grief must have communicated itself to Matt, for he gently hugged her, saying, "But I now know you're my Jilly Dilly. Come, let's get you settled in and have that bottle of champagne." He turned to the younger man. "Lance, come in after you put the car away. I'll be in the library."

Then he led Jill into the house, his arm still affectionately wrapped around her waist.

The house was large and tastefully decorated. A wide sweeping stairway rose up the right side of the entry, and John was coming from the hallway at the top. As he tiredly plodded down the steps, he said, "The young lady's things are in the purple room."

"Thank you, John. Now, would you go down and get me a bottle of champagne? The very best we have."

"Champagne, sir?" the old man asked in surprise.

"Yes, John. Bring it to the library, please." Matt's eyes were twinkling as he drew Jill up the stairs after him.

A befuddled John left, for once without any grumbling remarks bobbing in his wake.

Chapter Three

The purple room, in spite of its name, was predominantly white, but with accents of lilac. It was an extremely feminine room with white-painted wicker furniture and a large white oval fringed rug in the center of its wooden floor. The bed, and the two windows which flanked it, were decorated with material that had lilac nosegays on a white background. Grass-green throw pillows on the bed and wicker lounger picked up the color of the leaves of the nosegays. It was a thoroughly professional decorating job, and when her uncle led her into the room, Jill gasped in surprise.

"Why, Uncle Matt, it's beautiful. But whose room is it?"

"It's yours, sweetheart."

"Well, yes, I know. But I mean, whose room is it regularly? Am I putting someone out?" Jill turned anxiously to her uncle. Anyone who had this room would not have wanted to give it up, and with no knowledge of who actually made up her uncle's household, Jill wanted to make no unmet enemies.

Her uncle looked worried.

"Don't you like it, honey?" he asked.

"Of course! I adore it! Lilac is my favorite color, and lilacs are my favorite flowers. Why . . ." But she stopped suddenly, catching the satisfied glint in her uncle's eye. She turned slowly to survey the room. "Why, Uncle Matt," she breathed. "Is this all for me? But how . . ."

"Don't think just because I'm old or since it's been ten years that I didn't remember my Jilly Dilly's favorite things. Remember when we used to take walks and I always let you pick one lilac blossom from that Mrs. . . . What was her name?"

"Carstairs," Jill supplied with a grin.

"Yes, Carstairs. She had a lilac bush that hung over the picket fence, and I let you pick just one flower each time we went past it."

"Oh, Uncle Matt," Jill managed to choke out before the beauty and thoughtfulness of what he had done for her robbed her of speech.

"Why, Jill! Tears? Now, now. Come here." And he wrapped her tightly in his loving arms while she sobbed against his massive chest.

She got control of herself again, and he let her go.

"Come down after you've freshened up," he said gruffly. As he turned to go, he indicated a door to the side. "That leads to a bathroom, which you share with the room on the other side, but no one is occupying it." With a wink he returned downstairs, leaving Jill to explore the room, which now held a much more personal appeal.

To think that he'd actually had this room decorated for her. And that he'd remembered how she loved lilacs. It was incredible! Jill sighed in content. No one had shown this much concern since her mother, and she hadn't realized how very hungry she had been for it.

Against one wall stood a dressing table, its mirror framed by lacy wicker. The top of the table was covered with glass, and two lilac-colored lamps, with shades covered in the same material as the bedspread, stood on either side. The sun was beginning to lower, and she flicked one of the lamps on.

After she had unpacked and showered in the adjoining bath, which had been decorated in grass-green like the throw pillows, she stood before the mirror again, her slender, shapely legs visible beneath the plush green towel she had wrapped around herself sarong fashion. As she was deciding what to wear for dinner with her uncle, there was a knock at the door. Thinking it must be him coming to collect her, she padded to the door, opening it with a rueful smile.

"I'm afraid I took too long in that gorgeous bathroom, Uncle Matt. I . . ."

But it wasn't her uncle's warm blue eyes that were making a sardonic sweep of her barely clad body. Cool gray eyes completed their thorough appraisal before Lance said, "And I'm afraid your uncle"—and the inflection he gave the noun expressed his continued rejection of her relationship—"is tired from the exertion of welcoming you. I refused to allow him to make the trip back upstairs, and came for you myself. We'll be awaiting you in the library, which is at the foot of the stairs, to your left."

"What do you mean my uncle is tired out? He looks perfectly healthy to me, in spite of his age." Jill

31

wondered if Lance's explanation had been deliberately designed to make her feel like an outsider.

"Looks are deceiving, as I'm sure you're aware, Miss Taggert," he answered insinuatingly. "Your uncle"— that inflection again—"suffered a serious heart attack several years back and has tired easily ever since."

"How long ago was that?"

"Five years ago, to be precise. That's why he didn't attend your . . . father's funeral. He was in the hospital at the time." The information was delivered coldly, as if he felt she would not be in the least interested.

But she was. The belated grief she felt for Uncle Matt was real, and she paled slightly. Then another fragment of evidence of Lucy's coldheartedness fell into place. She had taken advantage of Matthew Lane's serious illness and probable resultant weakness to make her plea for money. She had been a heartless, clever con artist. The thought sent shock waves through her, and she swayed, staring blankly.

"Miss Taggert? Are you all right?" Lance's words came from far off.

"Yes," she responded faintly.

Lance reached out as if to steady her, but she had already gotten herself under control, even though, moments before, a nameless ache inside had made her want to accept his support. Fleetingly, the thought of how nice it would be to be wrapped securely in those strong arms, cradled against that broad muscular chest, slipped through her mind unbidden. Astonished at her own weakness, she dismissed it posthaste. Why in the world would she want to be held by such a sarcastic, caustic man? She didn't even like him! Abruptly she turned away.

"I'll be down as quickly as I can," she assured him.

"Good," he acknowledged shortly.

Jill closed the door on his retreating back, pondering her own reaction.

Finally, as she finished dressing and making up her face, which she did sparingly, she convinced herself that she was so hungry for security that she was willing to accept it from any quarter.

Only slightly comforted by this, she stepped out into the hall after surveying her appearance in the wicker-framed mirror. For her first night with her uncle in his gracious home she had chosen a lightweight sun dress with double spaghetti straps tied in bows at the shoulders above a pleated bodice that formed the gently gathered skirt. The dress was white with red piping along the top edge of the bodice, running fully around, front to back. Tiny red flowers were embroidered along the hem. With her feet tucked in cork-heeled white leather sandals, she felt totally in tune with her new surroundings.

The cork heels had crepe-rubber soles that further muffled her soft step on the carpeted stairs, so that as she neared the base of the stairway, she knew the men in the library failed to hear her approach. This was borne out by their raised voices, arguing about her. She paused, speechless, on the bottom tread as she heard Lance Darrel say, "I don't care about gut feelings, Matt. You always were a soft touch where women were concerned. But I still think she's a phony. Now that she's here, what have you got to lose by my starting an investigation like I wanted to in the first place?" His voice was intense, backed by strong emotion.

Her uncle's reply came slowly, as if he were tired of the whole discussion. "Now, you know how I feel about that, Lance. If I have to make a choice between believing Lucy and little Jill, I'll believe my niece."

"But is this big Jill the same as little Jill? Oh, granted

she's got blue eyes and black hair, but so have a lot of women."

"Ah, but not that shade of blue. Cornflowers, or a beautiful summer sky—"

"Don't start getting lyrical again," Lance interrupted irritably. "And don't let her obvious beauty blind you to the possibility that she could be an impostor. It's fairly easy to do." Lance's voice roughened.

Then he must have taken a drink, for Jill heard the chink of ice in a glass and her uncle caution, "What's gotten into you tonight, boy? I've never seen you drink with such a vengeance before. You won't be able to appreciate the fine meal Consuelo has made for tonight."

"I don't care about food!" Lance burst out. "I care about you, Matt, and I don't want to see you made a fool of again. Let me start an investigation—"

"No!"

"At least let me find out if Jill's death was reported in the local paper five years ago."

"Oh, Lance." Her uncle sounded as if he were beginning to weaken and tire.

Jill stepped off the last stair and turned to the left, entering the library, where she saw the two men on the far side of the room standing before a bar, facing each other. Lance's hand was clenched around a cocktail glass, looking as if he could crush it to splinters.

Her entrance startled them, and their eyes shifted to each other momentarily, the question of how much she'd heard expressed inaudibly.

"Why don't you let him do it, Uncle Matt? And while you're at it, Mr. Darrel"—she approached him boldly, her expression aggressive—"why don't you check into Lucy's death, too. It was in the Topeka paper on November 25." Her eyes challenged his as she came to stand beside her uncle.

"Now, sweetheart, you weren't supposed to hear all this," her uncle began, only to be gently interrupted by Jill.

She placed her small hand inside his big one, giving it a squeeze, and said, "No, Uncle Matt. I should have heard this. In fact, I'm thankful I did. You see, your Mr. Darrel has already thrown down the gauntlet. He accused me of being an impostor at the airport."

Lance scowled, his eyes throwing darts that failed to quell her. She went on confidently.

"Impostors can be fairly easy to prove false, can't they, Mr. Darrel?"

He nodded tersely.

"So I suggest you get on with your investigation. I'd like this matter cleared up even more than you would, which I'm sure is considerable," she remarked, returning his sarcasm in good measure.

Lance looked at Matthew. "Well?" he prompted.

"Oh, all right. All right," he gave in reluctantly. "But why can't people just trust each other?" he added petulantly.

"You trusted Lucy five years ago," Lance reminded him darkly. "And look where you are now."

The old man flinched at the younger one's reproof. "Yes," he agreed sadly. "To think that I mourned my Jilly Dilly when I needn't have." He regarded Jill fondly.

Love choked her response, but she expressed herself more eloquently than words could have by throwing her arms around his neck and pressing a fervent kiss on his pale cheek. She could see now that there were signs of fatigue she hadn't noticed before. Tiny lines etched his brow and radiated from the corners of his eyes. The edges of his mouth drooped slightly, and his face looked somehow more haggard than when she'd arrived. Compunction over the part she'd played in his exhaustion made concern accent her soft voice as she urged him to sit down.

"Come sit with me on the couch over there, Uncle Matt."

He went with her willingly, a sigh of content escaping his lips as he settled beside her.

"Would you like a drink, Miss Taggert?" Lance asked tonelessly.

It was apparent that, for the present at least, they were to observe a truce or armistice until his investigation was completed. Jill wondered how he would treat her when he found out that she had been telling the truth.

"A gin and tonic, please, Mr. Darrel," she requested in the same politely impersonal manner he had used.

"Now, there's a good drink for the weather," her uncle approved. "Make that two, Lance." Then he remembered something. "Oh, but the champagne I had John bring up."

"Uncle Matt"—Jill laid a hand on his arm—"please, let's wait until after Mr. Darrel's investigation is completed. Then we'll have something to celebrate." Her voice communicated her confidence in the outcome, and her uncle smiled.

"That's an excellent idea, Jill. Yes, let's do that. Lance, what do you think?"

Jill's glance met Lance's speculative gaze. He, to the contrary, was sure of her defeat. That was apparent in the tone of voice he used in his agreement. "Certainly, Matt. We'll definitely wait." But only Jill was aware of the undercurrents in his answer.

His glacial regard of Jill did more than chill her blood. She felt her nerves freezing under the cold penetration of those compelling eyes, and had to drop her gaze to her lap. She wondered anew at this previously unexperienced reaction to a man. Men of any sort had failed to affect her in the past. Lucy's escapades with members of the opposite sex had made Jill's view of them slightly jaundiced. As a result, she had won the reputation of being the Frozen Virgin in high school. Her cool, aloof manner had been a barrier no boy her age had bothered to breach. So as yet, her experiences with men were minor and had left her totally unprepared for dealing with a man like the dark, sardonic Lance Darrel. His looks alone were imposing, and it had only been by allowing herself to be swept on a tide of righteous indignation that she had had the temerity to confront him earlier.

She watched him now through her lowered lashes as he bore her drink across the room. He had changed into a light gray leisure suit, with a muted-pattern shirt underneath. He wore no tie, and the top two buttons of his shirt were undone, the collar spread to lie flat over the lapels of his suit. There were dark curling hairs just visible at the bottom of the V formed by the spread collar, and Jill found herself uncomfortably affected by the sight.

With slightly trembling fingers, she took the tall drink he held out to her and some of it spilled on her dress.

"Oh!" she exclaimed, and before she could react further, Lance had whipped out a clean handkerchief and was offering it to her, his expression sardonic. "Thank you," she murmured, embarrassed both by her clumsiness and by her indebtedness to him for his assistance. She dabbed at the spot briskly. Fortunately, only a small amount had spilled and she was able to sop it up quickly. Lance held out his hand for the cloth, and after a moment's hesitation she returned it, eyes downcast.

John came in, saving her more embarrassment, and announced dinner in his grumbly voice.

As they walked out into the hallway, her uncle leading the way, he said, "Remind me to show you around the house after dinner, Jill."

"Yes, I'd like that, Uncle Matt." She nodded, tucking her arm through his, and he led her into the dining room.

It was tastefully decorated, with a high ceiling like the rest of the house that Jill had seen so far. Her uncle seated her at the side of the Queen Anne table, and he and Lance sat at the two ends.

His cook, Consuelo, who was of Puerto Rican extraction, bustled in with John close on her heels, to serve the excellent dinner she had prepared, then disappeared after being introduced to Jill.

As they ate the delicately seasoned fillet of sole in shrimp sauce, the conversation was carried on almost exclusively by Jill and her uncle. Lance ate in silence, unnerving her by his continued scrutiny. She wasn't sure what he was looking for and felt the probing of that brooding look acutely. She tried not to let it affect her as she answered Matt's questions on her life with Lucy and the factors that led to Lucy's death.

After dinner the promised tour of the house was conducted. It had been built in the thirties, when Matt had first moved from the northeast and had wanted a home that would remind him of his old one in New

England. It was large for one man, with not only the library and dining room on the first floor but also the kitchen, a living room, a bath, and another room he used as an office.

Throughout were the high ceilings, many windows to provide views of the ocean by day and to admit the cooling ocean breezes by night, and the furnishings were old and homey-looking, like the ones Jill's mother had collected. She found herself feeling very much attracted to the place her uncle had lived in for forty years.

She found out that John had been employed back then and had stayed on through depression, war, and recession. A true friend in distress and good times alike. Jill could better understand why her uncle tolerated his slightly surly attitude.

What she didn't understand was Lance's place in all this. As her uncle conducted the tour of the second floor, which comprised six bedrooms and two full baths, she tried thinking of a subtle way to question him.

John, Matt, and she occupied three of the bedrooms —Consuelo lived with her husband on the grounds in a cottage—and one of the remaining three bedrooms was also occupied. As her uncle gestured through the open door at the masculinely furnished room, he explained, "And this is Lance's."

The room was at the end of the hall, opposite Jill's. As she stared at the interior with its natural oak furniture and muted browns and grays, she was unable to contain her curiosity any longer.

"Lance's!" she echoed. She was thankful they had left him downstairs after he declined accompanying them on the tour, for she was sure she would have been unable to refrain from making some comment even in his presence. "He lives with you, Uncle Matt? But why?"

Her uncle fixed her with gentle regard, his eyes melancholy with deep thought. "Because," he said softly, "he's my son."

Chapter Four

The gorgeous Florida sunshine was streaming in through the curtained windows, the warming rays barely able to penetrate the deep slumber that held Jill locked in a world of dreams. She rolled over, and a slanting ray probed her sleep-drugged lids, causing her to blink and open her eyes bemusedly. Just for a moment she forgot where she was, both in location and stream of time, and she wondered why she was able to smell the rich aroma of coffee when she hadn't risen yet to perk it.

"Good morning, Jill," Consuelo greeted her as she set an attractive tray beside the bed on the nightstand. It had been her entrance into the room that initially woke Jill, and she drew the curtains back, allowing the sun to fully explore the room.

The action brought Jill completely awake, and she sat up, admiring the single hothouse rose displayed in a tall cut-crystal bud vase.

"Oh, Consuelo, you shouldn't have done all this," she protested in embarrassment. "I'm not used to being waited on." Remembering all those lonely mornings of rising, preparing her own breakfast, and checking to see if Lucy had made it home the previous night, then leaving for school, her face clouded.

"Then get used to it, young lady," Consuelo counseled in motherly tones. "From what your uncle has told me, you deserve it. Catering to that woman . . ." she started to mutter, then brought herself up short at Jill's expression. "Well," she continued briskly, "you can just relax while you're here and be waited on for a change." She beamed at Jill, who couldn't resist the warmth and generosity of Consuelo's manner, and her face relaxed into an answering smile.

"Your uncle rises with the birds, and he's already had his breakfast," Consuelo continued. "But he said when you're ready, come join him in the office. Then you can go see the diving school." With that she bustled out, presenting the image of a small dynamo with perpetual motion.

Jill envied her early-morning energy, but only briefly, as she settled back, her pillow supporting her against the wicker headboard, and savored her first sips of the incredibly delicious coffee. Was there anything Consuelo couldn't make transcend the ordinary? she wondered in admiration.

The removal of the silver cover revealed a plate of eggs, bacon, and toast, along with hash-browned potatoes. Jill viewed the repast in alarm. Was she expected to eat all that? She'd better explain to Consuelo that she was certainly no lumberjack or field hand, just a toast-and-coffee person.

Then the full import of Consuelo's information penetrated her sleepy mind, and she bounded out of bed with uncharacteristic eagerness. Today she was going to have a look at Uncle Matt's scuba-diving school.

As she looked over her wardrobe for appropriate dress, she reviewed the discussion she'd had with her uncle after his surprising disclosure the previous evening. With a wry twist to her attractive mouth she remembered her reaction to her uncle's announcement that Lance was his son. Even as her heart had stopped due to some nameless anguish this revelation caused, the more reasonable part of her mind had fixed on the fact that the two men had different surnames. At the time she had refused to try to understand why the knowledge that she and Lance shared a blood relationship had such a devasting effect on her. However, that had quickly been removed anyway by her uncle's following rephrasing of his statement.

"Lance has been like a son to me, honey," he'd qualified. Then he'd explained about his sister Joan. She had married Jim Darrel and together they waited for the blessing of a child that never came. Finally, before Jim went off to take part in the tail end of World War II, they had opted for adoption, and little one-year-old Lance had come into their lives. He was two when his new father had entered combat in Europe, and Lance had never seen him again, as an undetected land mine had ended his father's life.

The close of the war had brought with it a housing shortage, and Joan had been forced to accept her brother's invitation to come live with him in his more than adequately roomy house. There they had lived in relative tranquility until Joan had been struck down by pneumonia, and its complications had taken Lance's second parent from him when he was only seven years old. From then on Matt, who had never married, became father and mother to him, raising him as his own. When he'd grown up, Lance became Matt's right-hand man, which at present entailed his being the manager and one of the diving instructors of Matt's scuba-diving shop and school, the one she was going to be shown today.

As she'd stood there in the hallway, hovering between her door and Lance's, listening to her uncle, she had found herself trying to visualize Lance as a boy, bereft of mother and father. Somehow the image of Lance as anything other than the dauntingly male individual he'd become was difficult to conjure up. Instinctively she knew Uncle Matt's attempts at taking the place of both parents wouldn't have been an unqualified success, in spite of his desire to do so and his loving, generous nature. She had experienced this bereavement, albeit later in life, and knew how that void remained unfilled.

After their discussion, her uncle reluctantly pleaded tiredness, excused himself, and went to bed. Jill balked at rejoining Lance downstairs. Choosing the coward's way out, she'd snagged John as he shuffled his way up the stairs and apologetically requested him to give Lance the message that both she and her uncle had retired. She'd fallen asleep almost instantly and never knew how soon Lance had followed them up. The room her uncle had so lovingly prepared for her caused a restfulness on her senses that almost drugged her with contentment.

Now she stood with growing anticipation in front of the closet. Obviously casual wear was dictated, and she withdrew a pair of faded but much-loved denim jeans and a pale blue T-shirt with tiny crocheted borders on the lower edges of the short sleeves and neckline. Pulling the soft T-shirt over her head, she glanced toward the view seen through the open curtains. As she tucked the bottom into the waistband of her snug-fitting jeans, she wandered over to gaze out the window.

Her arrival the previous evening hadn't allowed for her tour of the outside, and the early-setting winter sun had made it impossible to see out her windows prior to turning into bed. This first opportunity to glimpse her surroundings caused her blue eyes to widen in delight. Her great-uncle's property was immense, with no other dwelling in sight, just an expanse of well-kept lawn ending where orange groves, their ripening fruit just turning color, bordered the two sides of the entry drive. She couldn't see toward the rear of the house, but a bright sliver of sun-dappled water indicated the ocean wasn't too far away. She noted the faintness of the ocean's roar, wondering why her uncle would choose to place his house so far from the shore. What was the point of living on ocean frontage without the benefit of the somnolent melody of the restless sea to sing one to sleep? Deciding that was just one of the many questions she wanted answered, she turned back to the room to finish dressing.

Shuffling into brown leather loafers and slinging a warm cardigan over her shoulders, she grabbed the tray, feeling slight guilt that its contents, except for the coffee, remained untouched and unappreciated. She took it downstairs to the kitchen and apologized profusely to Consuelo, who eyed the rejected tray with disfavor. After assuring the affronted cook it wasn't her cooking at fault but Jill's own lack of appetite in the morning, she went in search of her uncle. She smiled in remembrance of Consuelo's comment dryly made as her black eyes darted assessingly up and down Jill's slight figure.

"No wonder you look like an underfed chicken," she muttered, and making clucking sounds like the mentioned fowl, she took the tray and went about her business.

A long hallway ran from the front door past the base of the stairs to the back of the house, ending in the kitchen. The living room, dining room, library, and office had doors opening off from it, and an archway defined the meeting of the living room with the dining room. The library and office each had double French doors leading to a shared covered porch, which ran the entire length of one side of the house.

When Jill entered the office, she found the room empty but the French doors wide, admitting slightly salt-tanged breezes. She went on out the doors, past white gauze curtains fluttering gently, and spied her uncle on the porch with Lance, both men comfortably ensconced in padded wicker chairs. The porch was covered with outdoor carpeting, its short pile muffling her steps, and as she left the confines of the office, she felt her skin prickling as she experienced that uncanny feeling a person has when he seems to be reliving a part of his past.

Her uncle and Lance were having a disagreement, and, as the night before in the library, the source of their contention was Jill. She had time to hear one disgruntled remark from Lance's lips before he was the first to notice her.

"Why can't you get Dougherty to show Jill around? I've quite a lot of work to do." Whatever her uncle's reply would have been was lost forever as Lance's cold eyes fell on Jill's hesitant form, poised just outside the office doors. "Good morning, Miss Taggert." There was little warmth in his greeting, which was only an attempt to satisfy the dictates of convention.

Her uncle turned in his chair, his craggy face wreathed in a smile of genuine welcome. Jill fixed her attention on it in hopes the warmth of his smile would thaw the chill induced by Lance's cold acknowledgment.

"Jill! Good morning, sweetheart." He patted a chair beside his to indicate his desire to have her sit there. "Did you sleep well? Have you had breakfast?"

Jill's mouth smiled in answer to his welcoming manner, but her eyes darted nervously to Lance. Why did he have to be there to ruin her first morning? In spite of her agitated thoughts, her voice was normal as she dropped into the chair and answered her uncle's questions.

"Yes, I did sleep well. But, no, I didn't eat. I'm afraid I don't eat breakfast too often, and besides"— her eyes slid involuntarily to Lance's as she phrased the ncxt statement, wanting to observe his reaction—"I was too excited about seeing your diving school to eat."

She was rewarded by a scowl as Lance sipped the cup of coffee held in one lean tanned hand. How could her uncle miss the undercurrent of dislike Lance had for her? she wondered as she returned her attention to him. Then, again, maybe he didn't, she mused, as a flicker of concern crossed Matt's face as his eyes too fell on the younger man's taut expression. Then it was wiped away as he looked at his grandniece with affection.

"Excited, are you? Good. I was just asking Lance to conduct you on the tou   I'm afraid I'm having one of my little spells, and he feels I should stay around home today."

Jill was instantly alert. "Little spells, Uncle Matt? What do you mean?" Her voice was husky with worry. Had they to do with the heart attack Lance had so chillingly told her about?

Confirming this suspicion, her uncle replied, "Unfortunately, my heart acts up from time to time. I have a condition caused by an attack several years back, and as a result, sometimes I get little flutterings that seem to bother everyone but me." He delivered this information unconcernedly as his gentle blue eyes met Lance's cool gray ones.

"What kind of a condition, Uncle Matt?"

"Arrhythmia. It's an extra or irregular heartbeat," Lance answered brusquely, perhaps feeling Matt would minimize its seriousness. "I take his blood pressure and pulse every morning, and today his pressure was slightly raised, and the extra beat was in evidence. He's on medication for it, and I want him to rest."

His answer was delivered in that hateful manner that made Jill feel like an unwanted, disinterested party. Her dislike for this man was beginning to well up inside her like a poison. She wanted to do something violent to him, something that would shake him out of his self-righteous complacence. Striving to school her features and calm down, she was unable to keep from casting one venomous look in Lance's direction before concentrating solely on her uncle. Lance was unperturbed by her look, even appearing slightly more complacent, as if he could read her mind and was fully aware of the disquieting effect he had on her. Obviously it pleased him to be able to affect her so adversely, and Jill made a solemn vow not to let him see one iota of the disturbance he caused her again.

"Now, Lance," Matt muttered deprecatingly, "you make me sound like I'm ready for the rest home. And the day I'm so invalided I have to spend my days lying around uselessly is the day I hope to die."

"Uncle Matt!" Jill exclaimed. "Don't say that," she pleaded in shock, her blue eyes large and luminous from the mere thought of losing him after just finding him. She rose to kneel at his side, and wrapped her arms around him, saying, "I don't have to see the school today. We can wait until you're feeling better."

"Now, that's ridiculous! You run along with Lance. Don't let an old man's silly little problems keep you down. I want you to see the school. I want to hear what you think of it. Now, go!" he ordered in mock gruffness.

Lance's mouth twisted sardonically, and he rose to tower over Jill's bent form. "Perhaps Miss Taggert has no wish to have me as a stand-in for your decidedly more welcome company."

His remark was a deliberate attempt to make her look petty and childish, and since she was already feeling ashamed of herself for allowing him to see the way he made her feel, she wasn't going to let him get the best of her again.

Straightening, she gave her uncle's shoulder a gentle squeeze and looked Lance straight in the eye, which took considerable effort. "Not at all, Mr. Darrel. I'd love for you to conduct the tour. I'm sure you'll do a thorough job." The words were innocuous enough, but her accompanying expression relayed her knowledge of what he was doing, and that she accepted the challenge.

"Oh, come now, you two. Stop being so formal," her uncle chided. "Call each other by your first names. Isn't it a little silly when you're going to be living in the same house?" His troubled blue gaze flicked from one to the other.

"Shall we leave, Jill?" Lance's use of her name came out stiffly, but it produced the desired effect on Matt Lane.

"That's better," he approved heartily, looking at Jill, who nodded.

"Yes, Lance." Her answer was barely less stilted

than his had been, and she forced herself to keep the smile she had fixed on for the benefit of her uncle until she had at least followed Lance from the porch. Then her mouth thinned in irritation as she trailed after Lance's erect form to the large garage at the back of the house. Trying to keep up with his ground-eating strides was impossible, and she slowed to her own natural pace. Let him wait, she thought angrily. It was obvious he didn't welcome her company, and nothing she did was going to alter that.

She glanced around her absently as she continued toward the car Lance was already backing out of the garage. The undercurrented exchanges she had with him always seemed to rob her of the interest and joy in discovering her new surroundings. Yesterday in the car she had barely seen the countryside flowing by, and she determined that today she was going to correct that.

The land seemed almost completely flat, or at best was gently undulating hills. The orange groves made it impossible to really see what it looked like. The sound of the distant ocean was louder now that she was outside, and she noticed a sand-colored track leading in that direction from the side of the house. Perhaps that was how one reached the beach. She would have to ask her uncle later. She ought to be carrying around a pad and pencil for writing down all the questions, she thought wryly to herself, and the smile teasing the corners of her mouth from that thought drew notice from Lance. As he opened the door for her, his gaze fell on her lips, and one dark eyebrow cocked quizzically as she slid into the Mercedes' elegant beige interior. Let him put whatever construction on that he wanted, she decided. Everything she said or did appeared to be suspect to him anyway. But despite her attempt at unconcern, she still felt a nervous tension begin to build somewhere deep inside.

Averting her head from Lance's unsettling presence, she stared out the window as he smoothly put the car in gear and accelerated down the driveway back toward the highway. As they passed the house, Matt Lane could be seen standing on the front steps waving them off.

"Will he be all right alone?" Jill worried aloud as she returned his wave.

"Of course. John and Consuelo are there," Lance reminded her laconically.

"Oh, yes," she murmured, turning in her seat to face the window. For the duration of the trip she attempted to acquaint herself with the Florida landscape whizzing by, but it was difficult due to the man who was propelling the car down the highway like an express train late for its destination.

Once she turned in her seat to observe him from the corner of her eye. His gaze was glued to the road as if he were hypnotized, and his hands seemed permanently curled into a viselike grip on the leather steering wheel.

"Must you drive so fast?" Her slightly anxious comment broke into his reverie, but his only response was a clipped "No" and a decrease in speed.

Jill gave herself back to contemplation of the view, sighing inwardly at the impossibility of getting along with this man. Forcing her attention on the landscape, she allowed her naturally inquisitive nature to surface, and began sopping up impressions of her surroundings.

The land was mostly flat, but covered with pocket-sized forests of pine trees and surprising clusters of tall, scruffy-looking palm trees. Here north met south and lived equably. They were nearing Daytona now, and the open, almost prairie land began to give way to civilization. Homes, mostly small affairs of either stucco or wood siding, began to fill her range of vision. Not all of them were well-kept-up, but in spite of their slightly neglected appearance, there were bright splashes of color. In front of many of the dwellings there were tall plants growing in bushlike hedges, and their five-pointed red flowers drew a frown of confusion on Jill's forehead. Turning reluctantly toward Lance, she pointed out the window.

"Those bushes with the red flowers—they look like poinsettias, but they're too big."

For the first time in their association, Lance's harsh features softened. Even smiling slightly, he answered, "They are poinsettias. You're used to the small plants you see at Christmastime, but here in our temperate weather they can be used for ornamental outside plantings, and they thrive quite well. If you look, you may see some which people have planted against high fences that grow to heights of six feet."

"Really?" Jill responded in wonderment, but it was wonderment more at his change of attitude toward her than at the interesting fact.

He looked at her a long moment. Then, as if he were remembering who she was, that implacable facade returned to blot out the warmth of before. Jill mourned its passing, gazing forlornly out the window.

"We're almost there," he informed her blandly.

She could do nothing more than nod her understanding. For some reason, she'd lost the ability to speak, and to her chagrin, she realized it was due to his snub. Why couldn't that moment of putting aside their personal differences and mistrust have lasted longer?

But that natural ebullience she possessed when experiencing something new once again reasserted itself, and she sat up expectantly as they turned down a paved road, its shoulder composed of sandy soil, and headed for the beach. A small sign announced their imminent arrival at Lane's Dive Shop. Smaller print below stated that diving instruction was also available.

Jill began to feel like a schoolchild being taken on a field trip. Unknowingly, she looked the part, her hands gripped in a knuckle-whitening clasp, her blue eyes bright with suppressed excitement, and a faint flush rouging her cheeks.

As he entered a blacktopped parking area, Lance's gaze fell on her a moment, and the sight arrested his attention. Then, with an almost vicious wrench of the wheel he guided the expensive car into a slot and roughly applied the brake. Jill's eyes snapped to his face in astonishment. Now what? She hadn't even said anything. Perhaps just her presence in the car was an unwelcome irritant to him. If that was the case, it could be quickly remedied, she thought grimly, letting herself out of the car swiftly.

As Lance's lean athletic body swiveled out, he remarked dryly, "Are you always that independent?"

"What?" Jill's lovely face expressed innocence of understanding, presenting an appealing picture that tightened his mouth into a grim line. He jerked his head in the direction of the side of the car she'd just vacated as he slammed his door with a solid-sounding thump.

"Don't you ever allow a man to open doors for you?"

Jill accepted the challenge she saw in his expression and said in what she hoped were crushing tones, "Frankly, I didn't think you'd care to."

"Touché, Miss Taggert," he murmured as he swept by her like an onrushing tide and headed for the front door of the shop. He was dressed in a black pullover and dark blue jeans, casual attire that made him seem somehow larger and more menacing than ever.

As she followed him, Jill couldn't help but observe the way he walked—"swaggered" was more like it—with a tight-hipped rolling step that made his shoulders alternately thrust forward. She was sure he'd have no trouble elbowing his way through a crowd if he felt so inclined. People would take one look at those impressive shoulders and voluntarily step aside.

These thoughts effectively prevented her from looking over the outside appearance of the building, and before she entered the door Lance was holding open for her—naturally with a sardonic quirk to his lips—she had time only for a brief impression to filter in. It was one-story, built of natural wood and stucco, with only one window facing the parking lot. But as she entered the shop, she saw it was flooded with light from an entire back wall composed of one massive plate-glass window.

Sparkling beyond, its gleaming surface heaving and thrusting, was the Atlantic Ocean. Jill stopped in awe, then walked slowly and reverentially up to the window, her rounded blue eyes mirroring the brilliant hue of the sky overhead. She'd never seen the ocean, only pictures or seascapes. The real thing was so much more awesome than she'd expected.

"It's so wild," she breathed, feeling somehow that the description was inadequate and even inane.

"It's choppier today than normal," Lance observed from somewhere behind her left shoulder. She thought he was like some big jungle cat, able to steal up behind his quarry undetected. "We're in for a change of weather, I think," he predicted.

Jill found speech impossible as she gazed immobile at

the churning, diamond-spattered water. Suddenly she felt an unreasonable urge to be out there, standing in the water up to her hips, allowing that pounding surf to engulf her.

As if he sensed her thoughts, Lance asked, "Would you like to go down there?"

"Could we?" Jill turned delightedly to him, pleased that he'd suggested exactly what she really wanted.

"Certainly. Come on." He took her arm and led her to a sliding glass door at the right of the huge window-wall, and led her out to a long deck that ran the length of the rear of the building.

Chapter Five

Seconds later she was standing before the most majestic scene she'd ever witnessed. She was glad of the sweater she'd brought, since the weather, which just a short time before had been fairly warm, was beginning to become blustery and the temperature was rapidly dropping. However, the delicious shivers dancing over her skin were not due to chill, but the ferocity of feeling she was experiencing, standing there at the edge of the sea, her nostrils tingling with the scent of salt and seaweed, with the pounding surf echoed by an equal pounding in her blood.

She felt the skin tightening on her face, something that always happened when she was having some soul-shaking experience. She closed her eyes, imagining what it would be like to be blind and to know the sea only by the sound of the waves crashing on the beach and the feel of the sand vibrating under her feet.

Stretching her arms wide, unmindful of Lance's

reaction, Jill cried, "I'm in love with it." And before he knew what she was doing, she'd kicked off her loafers and was racing into the waves, laughing and free like a child let on the loose.

"Jill!" Her name exploded in a roar, but she paid no heed and waded in up to her knees.

Unfortunately, having no knowledge of the ways of the sea, she failed to realize the dangerous repercussions of that ebb and flow that thrilled her. One moment she was standing erect; the next, the force of the undertow was sending her downward. Strangely, she didn't even mind the idea of getting soaked, and she held out her hands to embrace the water.

Before she actually touched the top of the next wave with the tips of her fingers, her body was snatched up in two iron-clad arms and held clamped to Lance's chest.

"Of all the idiotic things to do," he berated her. "I should have let you be pulled out by that undertow, but I'm not *that* cruel." He marched through the surf and partway up the beach, his jaw clenched in anger, his eyes like white-hot shards of steel.

Jill swallowed convulsively and stared into Lance's face, so close to hers. Up close she could see a nerve twitching along his clamped jaw, and with a sinking heart she realized that her impetuous action had furthered the breach between them. She was about to formulate an apology, when Lance swung her down from his arms, depositing her neatly to stand firmly on the beach, before she could voice it.

The ease with which he disposed of her body made Jill think he'd be perfect cast as Tarzan in a Hollywood movie. Instantly the image of him swinging from vine to vine, effortlessly transporting his Jane, flickered across the screen of her mind, and a giggle bubbled up before she could suppress it.

Lance was bent over, having removed his shoes and socks, and was squeezing excess moisture from his sodden pants legs. He raised his head to peer up at her.

"You dare to laugh at my predicament after I may have just saved your precious little life?" he accused furiously. The twin barrels of his anger-filled gaze trained on her startled face.

"Saved my life?" she countered incredulously.

"Yes, Miss Taggert." Lance stood erect, his hands on his lean hips. The tautness of his stance matched the tone of his voice as he continued. "It may interest you to know that many people who are unfamiliar with the ocean's tricks—especially on a stormy day like today— have been pulled under by the strong current produced by each wave as it recedes. They are so surprised they don't react properly, some even open their mouths, and I'm sure with your imagination you can figure out what happens next." Jill looked about to object; Lance cut her off with: "And I'm not talking about beginners; I'm talking about excellent swimmers who are experienced only with placid pools or lakes. The first thing you'd better learn about the ocean, young woman, is to respect its power." His castigation flowed over her head as the ocean might have done minutes before but for his fast action.

"Yes, Mr. Darrel," she responded meekly. "But I am one of those excellent swimmers you talk about. I was on the school swimming team at home and qualified for a national all-school final," she added in a flash of temper which subsided as she remembered the reason she hadn't been able to compete in those finals. Lucy had progressed to the point where she couldn't be left alone overnight. After Jill's father died, Lucy had gone from a closet alcoholic to a full-blown out-in-the-public-eye one. She'd become the talk of the town, and the thorn of Jill's existence.

Unfocusing from these torturous memories, she found herself staring into Lance's intent face. Just for a moment something flickered in his eyes; then abruptly he bent down, retrieving his shoes and socks, and started for the shop.

"There are some towels in the office we use to dry off with," he threw back, and Jill plowed along through the fine white sand after him, subdued again.

As she trudged back up the weathered steps leading to the large deck, she noticed for the first time a tall redwood enclosure. A gate was opened wide, permitting Jill to glimpse an Olympic-size pool, its calm azure water an insipid and uninspiring view after seeing the tumultuous Atlantic. Jill wondered why her uncle would have a pool when the more exciting prospect of swimming in the ocean beckoned. That was another question to add to the steadily growing list she was mentally compiling.

Lance strode into the shop, heading for a door at the side, the upper half of which was a glass window. Grasping the doorknob, he glanced back at Jill, who was now taking in the details of the shop, and thrust it open, entering the room beyond without waiting for her to catch up.

She heard him speaking to someone but was too interested in the shop, with all its aquatic wares, to care what he was saying, or to whom. Now she was closer to things that interested her: swim fins, snorkels, masks, everything she was familiar with, and quite a lot she was not. There were racks of wet suits in all shapes, sizes, and colors. Fins in different lengths and types hung from the wall above a glass-enclosed case in which various makes of diving apparatus were displayed. An open counter divided the shop, where one could find masks, snorkels, and other diving needs.

Jill walked slowly past it, her bare feet making no sound, and stopped just short of entering the room that was obviously the office. There were two desks with chairs and a set of four tall filing cabinets. Directly before one of the file drawers was a woman bent over to retrieve one of the manila folders, her derriere presenting a view that Jill could only describe as voluptuous.

Lance was in a small bathroom at the side, procuring some thick white terry towels, and was saying, "I want that invoice mimeoed, Yvonne."

Yvonne—who could only be the secretary, Mrs. Flemming, Jill surmised—murmured her acquiescence. Jill thought both the parts of the figure she could see and the muffled voice clashed with her preconceived idea that her uncle's secretary would be elderly. The woman straightened, still with her back turned, and Jill saw that her hair was almost platinum blond. Then she pivoted toward the center of the room and Jill saw she was stunningly beautiful and somewhere in her late twenties. But above all that, her figure was superb from all angles. Its lushness made Jill feel exactly like Consuelo's undernourished chicken.

"Oh!" the secretary exclaimed, catching sight of Jill for the first time. "Are you Jill Taggert?"

The woman's eyes, a fathomless shade of dark brown, ran up and down Jill's figure as if she too were aware of the decided difference between them. Feeling scrawny and flat chested, Jill stepped into the room, only to open her mouth in acknowledgment and have Lance's cool voice intercede.

"Yes, Yvonne, this is Jill, Mr. Lane's long-lost niece." His tone was dry as he cast a deprecating glance over her bedraggled appearance. "Jill, this is Mrs. Flemming, who keeps the family business financially afloat by running this office as efficiently as a precision watch."

Yvonne glowed from this tribute, giving Lance what Jill thought could only be described as a sickeningly provocative look of gratitude. Was Mr. Flemming the recipient of such looks? she wondered. If so, it was a wonder Yvonne had the time to come to work.

"I'm to conduct a tour for Miss Taggert, but it shouldn't take long. Where's Scott?" Lance directed this question to the sultry secretary as he tossed a towel at Jill.

"He's in the back stowing the gear from his last lesson," Yvonne's low melodious voice explained as she perched on the edge of one of the desks, looking demurely up at Lance.

Jill watched her obvious play for him with disgust. If Mr. Flemming were a witness to this, she could be in for trouble. Lance seemed to be susceptible to her charms, for he smiled warmly down at her; then his gaze fell on Jill.

"Are you finished?" he inquired coolly.

Slipping into her loafers after removing the last grain of clinging beach sand, Jill stood up, answering, "Yes," and returned the towel to the bath.

"Let's go, then." Lance directed one last charm-filled smile toward Yvonne, saying, "I'll look at those invoices later," and led Jill back into the shop.

She felt the secretary's calculating gaze follow her from the room and unconsciously stiffened her spine. There was something so grating about being weighed up in the beauty balances and found lacking.

Lance paused in the center of the shop, turning to fix Jill with an ironic look. "Frankly, I don't see that there's much to explain." He waved his hand around, encompassing it all. "This is a shop. Those are Aqualungs. Those are wet suits. These are snorkels. These are fins. . . ." He kept up a running commentary as his long strides measured first one wall of the room and then the other, with Jill hard pressed to keep up. She would have liked to talk in more detail about the various items, but it was apparent Lance's intention was to make his explanation of the shop perfunctory.

Lance had come to a halt at a door marked "Dressing Room," and looking to see if Jill had caught up with him, he nodded toward the door. "In there is where the diving students get changed for their lessons. It also leads to our storerooms, both for new merchandise and for stowing used and rented gear."

Needing something to say, instead of looking like a dim-witted deaf-mute, Jill asked, "What's the pool I saw outside for?"

"For beginning diving lessons and for days when the ocean is too rough." Again, that deadpan delivery, but before Jill could foolishly make some caustic remark, the door marked "Dressing Room" swung out and a tall, blond, darkly tanned man stepped out. He was only one or two inches shorter than Lance, but was fully as wide, with the muscular torso of an athlete. He was also extremely good-looking, almost perfectly so, and the grooves at the sides of his mouth deepened as he greeted Lance.

"L.D.! Good morning. A little late today, aren't you?" Then his green-brown eyes noted Jill's presence. "Ah, could this be the reason?"

His warm easygoing manner soothed Jill's ruffled nerves, but it seemed to produce the opposite effect on Lance's.

"This is Mr. Lane's grandniece, Jill Taggert," he

explained shortly. "Miss Taggert, Scott Dougherty, our illustrious diving instructor. If you have any more questions of a specific nature, perhaps he can answer them."

Right then Yvonne stuck her gorgeous head out the office door, calling, "Lance, there's a phone call for you."

With a grim set to his face, Lance turned, leaving Jill without so much as a nod, and headed for the office. To her amazement, as she watched his retreating back, Jill heard Scott jibe softly, "Oh-oh! It's Captain Bligh at the helm again, I see."

Jill's startled blue eyes darted to his, noting the disarming smile he was bestowing on her.

"And what," he continued in a teasing vein, "did our little niece from Kansas do to him to get him so surly this morning?"

"Me?" Jill protested with a laugh, but she knew Scott Dougherty had accurately put the blame on her. The smile on her lips slipped a little as she acknowledged, "I'm afraid you're right, Mr. Dougherty, I—"

" 'Scott,' please," he insisted.

Jill nodded. "Scott. He and I haven't exactly hit it off since I arrived."

"Which was?"

"Yesterday afternoon."

"Much too short a time to write someone off, don't you think?" Scott questioned with a twinkle in his eyes that caused the corners to crinkle attractively.

"I'm not sure I understand your meaning." Jill was confused. Was he implying that she was too quick to condemn Lance, when in actuality it had been the other way around?

"I mean, if L.D. is so foolish as to rub you the wrong way, that's his problem. I, for one, am only too happy to welcome you with open arms. Figuratively, of course," he bantered.

Jill visibly relaxed. Now, here, at least, was a man full of that southern charm that was so touted. "Would you . . . er . . . have the time to explain some of the equipment to me?" she asked hesitantly.

"Didn't Lance . . . ?"

"No." Jill shook her head eloquently.

Scott proceeded to correct that situation for the next half-hour, explaining in some detail about scuba gear and its use. Jill began to grow excited. Learning to dive was sounding extremely desirable, and when she wistfully expressed that desire out loud, Scott immediately offered his services as instructor.

"I'm sure your uncle would be delighted to see you take an interest in his favorite pastime," he remarked.

"You mean he dives?" Jill asked incredulously, never having considered for a moment that a man as old as her uncle would don suit, scuba gear, and flippers, and actually participate.

"Well, for the past five years his diving has had to be curtailed somewhat. Doctor's orders," Scott explained soberly. "But I've never seen such a case of sustained enthusiasm for any sport as your uncle has shown. Now he does it rarely, and only when both Lance and I are free to accompany him."

"Why is that?"

"He could have another heart attack at any time, and because of his size, it would take both of us to get him to the surface and back on dry land." Scott sighed heavily. "It's a crying shame, too, because diving has always been Matt's one true love. He was one of the people responsible for getting diving started toward its present popularity in this area. But I expect you know all this, hmm?" His warm green-brown eyes rested on

Jill then, and she noted one of them was just a shade browner than the other, making them an unmatched set. It was a discovery that kept her gaze riveted to his at the very moment Lance returned from the office.

"Have you finished, Dougherty?" he asked abruptly, causing Jill to start at the unheralded sound of his chilling voice. His pantherlike stride had brought him silently to her side.

Scott's look as he glanced at him revealed his surprise at his slightly hostile manner, but his voice was bland as he returned levelly, "Yes, I've just offered my services as diving instructor to Jill."

Those cold gray eyes came to rest with disturbing intensity on Jill's averted profile. She answered Scott's offer with as much enthusiasm as she could muster under the oppressing circumstances.

"I'll ask my uncle, and if he has no objections, we can start right away, can't we?"

"Tomorrow, if you like."

"Fine, I'll be here."

This interchange concluded, Lance and Jill headed back to the car. As he opened the door for her, he inquired, "Well, what do you think of the place?"

Without thinking, Jill voiced the first thought in her mind. "I didn't realize a small operation like this could be so profitable."

"What do you mean?" Lance's cool, appraising eyes sharpened on her, causing a shudder of unease to tauten her already painfully stretched nerves.

"Well, I mean the house, this Mercedes. It just doesn't seem possible that one could afford those things on the income from this." She waved her hand around, a weak flutter, indicating the shop.

Lance's mouth twitched, and Jill observed the muscle that jumped as he clenched his jaw, feeling a fresh wave of hysteria threatening to rise up and engulf her. What had she said now? Was there nothing she could say or do right? Nothing that would please this arrogant man?

"Your uncle bought a large amount of acreage when he first moved down here, Miss Taggert," he began explaining, his voice heavy with condemnation. "He also owns a share in an extremely profitable resort hotel in Miami. That, combined with the return from his citrus crops, forms the bulk of his wealth. This"—he swept a long-fingered hand out, encompassing the shop as Jill had done—"is more or less his hobby. Your uncle is not a stupid man. Something you'd do well to remember in the future." With that last caustic remark stinging her cheeks red, he whirled and strode toward the other side of the car.

The return trip to the Lane home was completed in chilling silence. In the future, Jill vowed, Mr. Lance Darrel was going to see as little of her as possible. And that, she realized, would be satisfactory to them both. In his eyes, she was condemned before proven guilty, a situation making it impossible for them to have a normal relationship. Therefore, avoidance was the best policy.

With this firmly decided, Jill fairly leaped from the car, not even looking back when Lance let her out at the front door. Then, with the gravel flying wildly under his tires, he accelerated down the drive.

As she slowly climbed the steps, attempting to give her tense body time to relax, she noted for the first time that there was another car parked in the semicircular drive that ran past the base of the steps. It was a fairly new one, and not an inexpensive model. Another of Uncle Matt's? Then Jill saw the letters MD on the license plate and a sharp stab of fear bit into her. Why would a doctor be here? Unless . . .

She raced up the remaining steps and thrust the door open just as a man dressed in casual wear but carrying a doctor's bag was descending the stairway. John was accompanying him, and the man was instructing him: "I want him kept in that bed for the remainder of the day, even if you and Consuelo have to take turns sitting on him."

John smiled tightly at that; then his glance fell on Jill, who had advanced toward the bottom of the stairs. Her face was very pale, and her already large blue eyes were enormous with unexpressed anxiety.

"Uncle Matt?" she managed to say, clutching the round ball-shaped finial at the base of the handrail.

"Nothing to worry about, Miss Taggert," John hastened to assure her. "This is Matt's old friend who just happens to be a doctor."

"Yes, indeed," the other man carried on, extending a hand to her, which she took with her own cold one. "I was just on my way to play golf, and since Lance called about that slight rise in blood pressure, I thought I'd stop by and see for myself. How do you do? My name's Tom Evans." He squeezed her hand encouragingly, revealing his undoubtedly reassuring bedside manner. He was near to retirement age, which classed him in that generation of doctors who had practiced in gentler, slower times, and even now found time to treat patients as whole human beings, body and mind, not as account numbers or by ailments. Dr. Evans would never refer to that "gall bladder" in room 103, Jill surmised. She liked him instantly and immensely, glad that her uncle had such a good friend and doctor rolled into one.

"Then he is going to be all right?"

"Certainly. Just a little bit too much excitement." The doctor's hazel eyes twinkled as he raised an admonishing finger. "And I'm sorry to say it's your arrival that's to blame," he accused gently. "Now, for your penance, you'll have to help Consuelo and John, here, sit on him all day. I want him resting in body, if not in mind."

"That's punishment I find extremely agreeable," Jill responded, smiling. "May I go up now?"

"You certainly may."

"Oh, good." Jill started up the stairs, then remembered her manners. "It was nice meeting you, Dr. Evans. I trust the next time we meet it will be strictly socially."

"Hear! Hear!" the doctor endorsed, and with John by his side, he went out the front door.

Jill found her uncle propped up in bed desultorily turning the pages of a magazine, which, as she got closer, was identified as a diving manual. The look on his face resembled that of a small boy who wishes to be out with his playmates, but instead is confined to bed by his mother and forced to take some bitter-tasting medicine. It brought a smile to her face, punctuated by the twin commas of her dimples.

"Jill!" Her uncle's haggard face was instantly transformed by her entrance. Patting the edge of his bed in an inviting gesture. he said, "Tell me all about your trip to the shop. What did you think of it?"

First giving him a hug, Jill did as she was asked, sinking gratefully down on the bed. She'd discovered that between her exposure to Lance and the meeting with the doctor, her legs had become weak excuses for support.

"It was very interesting," she began, and glossing over Lance's brevity and rudeness, she described her first reaction to the ocean, her interest in the equipment, the shop, and ended with Scott's offer to be her diving instructor.

As predicted, the old man practically glowed, his satisfaction with his niece's genuine enthusiasm radiating from his brilliant blue eyes.

"So you'd like to try diving, hmm? You'll not regret it. The world below the waves is beautiful, but you have to be a strong swimmer. Are you? Because you need to pass rigid tests to be allowed to take diving instruction," he cautioned, his face revealing his doubts that a girl raised in the Midwest would have much chance to become such.

"Oh, yes, Uncle Matt. That's just it. I was on the school swimming team and even since I graduated I swam regularly at the local YWCA. I know I can do it," she assured her uncle eagerly, her eyes sparkling. Right now in her life she knew she needed a sense of direction, a goal to aim for, and on the trip back in the silence of the Mercedes she had formulated a plan she even felt a little reluctant to tell her beloved uncle about. If she could pass the test, become a proficient diver, then— But her uncle's voice cut short the plottings of her mind.

"How come Scott offered to teach you? Didn't Lance?" There was the suggestion of a frown on his forehead and in his voice.

"Er . . . no, he didn't." She eyed him warily, hoping he wasn't going to be difficult. It didn't take much intelligence to figure out which of the two men her uncle would favor.

Matt Lane didn't appear happy about this.

"Lance is more experienced than young Dougherty," he said as if to himself; then his eyes lit on Jill, who was watching him with a growing sense of unease. "Perhaps if I speak to him he'll take you on instead of Scott," Matt Lane went on, and as Jill was opening her mouth to protest, he said, "It's not that I don't think Scott is a good instructor. I wouldn't hire him if he wasn't. But Lance is the best around, and I don't want to settle for less than the best where my Jill is concerned," he concluded affectionately, causing a lump to form in Jill's throat.

Touched as she was, she still felt he was being needlessly concerned, and the thought of having Lance teach her anything was horrifying. She attempted reasoning with the old man.

"But I've already told Scott yes, and we've made plans to start tomorrow. I can't tell him Lance is going to take his place without insulting his abilities as an instructor."

Her uncle was beginning to show signs of agreement, and she rushed on. "Besides, that's Scott's chief job, isn't it? So he would be more likely to have the time to devote to an extra student. But Lance is very busy running the shop, and to ask him to make room in his already overcrowded schedule seems thoughtless." She ended slightly out of breath and stared as expressionlessly as possible at her uncle, awaiting his reaction to what she thought had been irrefutable logic. She discovered she was holding her breath, and let it out carefully when Matt nodded his head and replied, "Yes, that's true. I guess you'll be in good hands." But he didn't sound totally convinced.

Using her uncle's heart condition as an excuse for making her escape before he could continue the uncomfortable discussion, she rose and squeezed the limp hand lying outside the blanket.

"Now, you know the doctor said to rest today. I'm going to peek in on you from time to time this afternoon and make sure that's just what you're doing."

"I think Tom gave me something to make me sleepy anyway," Matt grumbled, stifling a yawn.

"That's because he probably knew it was the only way to keep you down," Jill teased, and kissing him on the forehead, she left.

Chapter Six

Jill's decision to avoid Lance was easier made than carried out. His position in the house as Matt's son, in spirit if not physically, meant that the three of them dining together was unavoidable.

As they were seated around the table that evening, Matt informed Lance of Jill's intention of taking diving instructions from Scott. Aside from a fleeting look which conveyed nothing of his thoughts, there was no reaction to this announcement, but his brow darkened as Matt added, "You can take Jill over to the shop with you in the mornings, can't you?"

"Yes," he agreed, but Jill heard the reluctance in his voice.

Her nerve ends screamed at the prospect of being cooped up in the car with him for that seemingly interminable trip to the shop. If Lance continued his silent treatment, she couldn't bear it.

"Good!" her uncle was saying with satisfaction. He seemed oblivious of the tension between Jill and Lance and saw nothing wrong with throwing them together.

The following morning the drive to the dive shop was every bit as uncomfortable as Jill had feared. She was ready precisely at eight, just as Lance had instructed her. One thing, at least, he couldn't hold against her was tardiness. However, as he conducted her to the car, there wasn't even the suggestion of a thaw in his nature.

When they arrived at the shop, Jill, remembering his caustic observation the previous day, perversely remained in the car, thereby forcing Lance to get out, come around to her side, and let her out. There was a challenging glint to her eye as she sedately swung her legs out of the car and stood up, bringing her face within inches of Lance's. He caught the look and closed the door slowly and deliberately, never once taking his eyes off hers.

She was the first to break the silent duel, and lowering her gaze, preceded him into the shop.

"Here she is," Scott greeted her warmly as she swung open the outer door and walked in. "I see you're all set," he commented, catching sight of the tote bag she carried, which contained her swimming suit and bathing cap. "Good morning, L.D.," he added on a less enthusiastic note as Lance followed Jill into the shop.

"Scott," Lance acknowledged shortly with a curt nod, and left them immediately, heading for the office.

There was a tangible reduction of tension in the air with his departure, and Jill unconsciously sighed in relief.

"Tired already?" Scott asked humorously as his eyes keenly made a search of her face.

"No! I'm raring to go. What do we do first?" Jill fixed her attention solely on Scott, endeavoring to wipe all thought of Lance from her mind.

"Did your uncle tell you you have to pass a pretty rigid test before you can be allowed to take lessons?"

"Yes." She nodded.

"Good. Then first we'll go change into suits," he said, moving toward the door marked "Dressing Room."

After Jill had changed in the small ladies' locker room, she followed Scott, who now wore a white swimming suit and carried two large towels, out through the shop to the swimming pool. Jill's suit, the one she'd had as a teenager, was a coral-red one-piece with soft gathers at the sides ending in little ties above her thighs. It received an admiring glance from Scott, whose green-brown eyes took in how closely it conformed to her gentle curves.

"Nice," was all he said, but there was evident appreciation in his voice.

"Okay," he began once they were in the pool, "I'm going to tell you to perform certain tasks and we'll see how you do. First, I want to see you do the flutter kick without using your hands. Just swim straight across the pool."

When Jill had done this, Scott had her do the sidestroke and the breaststroke, and then, using a combination of all three strokes, Jill had to swim two hundred yards without taking a rest. This she was able to do easily due to her training as a swimmer in school.

"You're doing fine," Scott complimented her as she was demonstrating she could tread water for three minutes.

After she had proven she could swim underwater at

least ten yards without the help of a dive or push off from the side of the pool, he asked, "Getting tired?"

"A little," she was forced to admit. She was floating on her back, motionless, for the required five minutes.

"Well, we've been at it for forty-five minutes and I think that's it for today," Scott said as he lithely pulled himself out of the pool. He gave Jill a helping hand, hauling her out of the water.

"Is there more to the test?"

"Yes, but I think it's best if you do it tomorrow. You have to dive into the deep end of the pool and retrieve a five-pound weight from the ten-foot mark." He handed her a towel and started back to the dressing rooms. "Also, I'm going to give you a form that has to be filled out by a doctor, stating you are physically fit enough to take diving instruction." He grimaced wryly. "Of course, finding a doctor who can fit you into his schedule soon may be difficult."

"Maybe Uncle Matt's friend Dr. Evans could do it?" Jill suggested hopefully.

"Sure!" Scott replied with obvious relief. "If you can get him to do it right away, there won't be a delay in starting your instructions."

"When I get back to the house, I'll call him and see if he'll do it," Jill promised, and went into the locker room to change.

She was cold and shivering, and glad to be dressed in clothes again. The pool had been warm, but Lance's prediction of a change in weather had materialized into darkly clouded skies and a cooler mass of air moving in.

When she returned to the shop, Scott was already there talking to Lance, who stood jingling his keys, looking impatient. There was a couple in the shop going through the rack of neoprene diving suits, and as

Jill entered, Scott bid her good-bye and moved off to help them.

Lance's cool gaze ran over her, noting the damp tendrils the swimming cap had failed to keep dry. Jill hadn't bothered to put on makeup, knowing the pool water would have washed it off, and that, combined with her slightly dampened hair, made her feel as attractive as a wet floor mop. It made her answer sharply when Lance asked if she was ready to go.

"Of course I'm ready!" she snapped, then was acutely sorry as she caught the disapproving look Lance sent her.

He delivered her to the house in total silence. As Jill thanked him abruptly and charged out of the car, she decided she'd had about all she could take of Mr. Lance Darrel. Her nerves couldn't stand the strain of daily drives with that exasperating hunk of masculinity. She went in search of her uncle, and found him out on the side porch. After reporting on her first session with Scott, she voiced the question uppermost in her mind.

"Uncle Matt, isn't there some way I could drive myself to the shop? It seems ridiculous for Lance to have to upset his routine to transport me there and back."

"Well, not exactly, honey," he answered apologetically. "You see, I do have another car, but Lance insists there be one here for John to use in emergencies." He looked disgusted. "Of course, I think it's nonsense. But if something should happen to me, he wants a car on the premises in case it becomes necessary to use it. I don't know what he thinks ambulances are for," he muttered under his breath.

Despite her aversion to doing so, Jill had to agree with Lance's reasoning. In the fairly remote area Matt Lane lived in, a car was a necessity, not a luxury. And sometimes ambulances were known to be busy or far away. Quick action in her uncle's case in getting him to a hospital could mean the difference between life and death. Begrudgingly she had to admit Lance was truly looking out for the best interests of the man he obviously loved. Jill wondered what it would be like to be the woman he loved. Would he treat her with the same concern for well-being? This line of thought was disquieting, and she quickly thrust Lance from her mind and looked at her uncle.

"Do you think your Dr. Evans could give me a physical so I can begin diving instructions?"

"I'm sure he could. Why don't we call him?" Matt suggested, rising.

They went into the house and made the call. Dr. Evans agreed to see her that afternoon, and John drove them into Daytona Beach to his office.

Jill was found to be in perfect health, just as she expected, although the doctor did say she was a little underweight.

"You young girls are always trying to be skinny as reeds, when men don't even like that," he teased.

"Oh, Dr. Evans," Jill returned, laughing, "I'm too young to be thinking about men."

The kindly doctor pooh-pooed that. "Nonsense! Girls are always thinking about men, no matter what their age." The twinkle of his eyes said he was only jesting.

"Not this girl!" Jill said vigorously. But on the way back to the house she reflected that her attempt at denial had fallen flat. Lately, a certain man had been making inroads on her thoughts, with discomforting effect.

For the rest of the week Lance drove Jill in with him to the shop. By Friday she had passed all the tests and

Scott had her fitted out in her own scuba gear. They had completed two days of diving lessons, which Jill had found a delight. She had learned how to ditch and don her air tanks while underwater, how to tow a companion in the rescue technique, and many other vital skills.

At the end of their Friday session, Scott and Jill were standing at the edge of the pool, outfitted in fins, aqua lungs, and regulators. Scott was demonstrating the proper way to share the mouthpiece of the regulator in the technique of buddy-breathing. They were standing close, sharing the regulator, and Scott joked, "I've never had to do this on a dive, but with such a beautiful girl, I'm tempted to pretend on our first time out." His eyes twinkled as he drew her close.

"Oh, Scott," Jill laughed. "I'm not beautiful. You're just an incorrigible flirt," she accused.

"Mmmm," he murmured, and before she could react, he lowered the mouthpiece and pressed his lips to hers.

It was a gently questing kiss. Jill was stunned by the unexpectedness of it, and didn't react before a cold voice broke them apart.

"Is this a demonstration in mouth-to-mouth resuscitation, or are you just moving in faster than usual, Dougherty?"

Lance stood just inside the entrance to the pool enclosure, thunderclouds gathering on his brow that rivaled the real ones in the sky.

Jill moved away guiltily, but Scott looked only irritated at this intrusion.

"What do you want, L.D.?" he asked brusquely.

"It's time for lunch, and I thought I'd collect Miss Taggert. Your session has already lasted twice as long as normal." Lance's explanation sounded more like an accusation.

Scott glanced at his waterproof watch and raised his eyebrows in surprise. "So we have," he remarked. "Well, Jill, I guess that's all for today. See you tomorrow?"

"Tomorrow?" Lance interposed. "Isn't that a little irregular? You normally don't conduct instruction on Saturday."

A nerve jumped in Scott's jaw, but his answer belied any annoyance on his part. "Yes, that's true. But Jill and I have agreed we might as well devote as much time to her instruction as we can. She'd like to learn as quickly as possible."

Lance's reaction to this was an inscrutable look Jill's way.

She nodded at Scott. "Yes, tomorrow," she returned, unable to meet his gaze. She knew her face was flushed, and her legs were a little unsteady as she marched past Lance, head held high, and went to change.

In the car, the expected silence was more oppressive than usual. Jill sensed a tautness in Lance that was almost material, and when he suddenly pulled the car over to the side of the road, turned off the ignition, and swung to regard her with a brooding expression, it wasn't totally unexpected.

She knitted her fingers into nervous knots, but she refused to question him, putting on the appearance of blithe unconcern. With a dip into her unplumbed stores of courage she managed to meet his gaze.

Finally he spoke. "Don't get mixed up with Dougherty," he ordered in a voice that was low and implacable.

Jill's mouth dropped open unbecomingly, then snapped closed. This was ridiculous! Who did he think he was? Stuttering slightly in her agitation, she retorted, "Y-you've got some nerve! Who appointed you my social director? If I want to get interested in Scott, I will, and there is nothing—"

"Miss Taggert!" Lance coldly interrupted her tirade. "Scott is from California. He's only going to be here for four more months. Then he returns home to open his own shop. Any interest he may have in you would only be temporary. I don't think he's likely to give up his bachelorhood just yet," he remarked dryly.

Jill bristled, indignation accenting her reply. "Mr. Darrel, one kiss hardly constitutes a marriage proposal. Don't you think you're reading more into it than necessary?" Her eyes sparkled and flashed, and the hands in her lap formed themselves into tight little fists.

"I've seen Dougherty in action before, Miss Taggert," Lance went on with a thread of mockery in his voice. "And I'm sure you've had enough experience to know his type is seldom serious." Jill opened her mouth to object, but Lance continued, his tone becoming hard with contempt, "I suggest you remember your uncle is a very moral man. He doesn't need the added stress of worrying needlessly over your amorous affairs." Jill gasped and paled, seeing now what he was leading to. "So for Matt's sake, stay away from Dougherty beyond diving instruction!"

The order fanned the flames of Jill's anger, but she held herself in check as she answered sweetly, "Does that apply to your amorous carryings-on?" At Lance's blank look, she said, "I'm sure he wouldn't approve of any little flings you might engage in with a married woman, either."

"I don't get your drift."

Jill could see he didn't, and triumphantly went in for the kill.

"I'm referring to the blatant flirting you and Mrs. Flemming engage in." She underscored the married title, and sat back complacently, prepared to watch Lance squirm.

Instead, his brow cleared, and a sly smile formed on his masculinely carved lips.

"Ah! I see. Your moralistic accusations fall short, Miss Taggert. *Mrs.* Flemming is a widow." He delivered this information with a decided glint in his eye as Jill's eyes rounded, and she felt crushed.

"Oh," was all she could get out before the unfairness of the situation made her lose her voice. Angrily she turned toward the window, ready to be done with the whole conversation.

Lance apparently wasn't, for he said, "Well?" in a challenging voice.

"Well, what?" Jill flared ungraciously.

"I think an apology is due for casting unmerited aspersions on Yvonne's character."

Jill swung to look at him. "To whom?"

Lance looked disgusted, and turned on the ignition with a vicious wrench of the key. Throwing the Mercedes in gear, he eased out onto the highway.

"Miss Taggert," he said heavily, once the car was in motion, "I suggest you keep relations between you and Scott in clear focus. And think about Matt once in a while."

That last bit amounted to an accusation that Jill didn't care about her uncle, and she couldn't let it stand.

"I do care about Uncle Matt, Mr. Darrel. Much more than you give me credit for. And this whole conversation is ludicrous anyway, since the reason for it was a simple little kiss, which I just happened to be the surprised recipient of. I had no inkling Scott was going to do it. I wasn't kissing him back. And you barged in just as it started. So . . . so . . ." She stopped, realizing she'd been giving an explanation for something that was really no concern of his. Before he could make some caustic rejoinder, she snapped, "And it's no business of yours. I don't want to discuss it further!"

"Fine," he agreed evenly. Jill thought she saw the suggestion of a twinkle in his eye, but he was gazing straight forward, and she wasn't sure.

It was with a sense of immense relief that she saw the Lane home coming into view. No sooner had Lance braked before the front door than she was out of the car and heading up the steps without a thought for thanking him. Unfortunately her precipitate exit was halted by his hateful voice.

"Miss Taggert," he called dryly.

Jill turned reluctantly, and immediately felt foolish. He was holding aloft the bag that contained her wet swimming gear. With crimson cheeks she was forced to walk to his side and retrieve it from him, carefully avoiding his eyes.

"Thank you," she muttered, and retreated to the sanctuary of the house.

However, as she was proceeding up the stairs, the front door opened. With a startled look back, she saw Lance come in. His mouth twisted sardonically as he met her round-eyed gaze.

"Lunchtime, Miss Taggert. Remember?" he asked softly, then chuckled as he walked toward the back of the house, disappearing from view before she'd gathered her wits and could speak.

With dragging steps she headed for her room, wondering how she could avoid eating lunch without offending Consuelo or worrying her uncle.

She decided Lance would derive too much pleasure from her absence at lunch, which would place more importance on their little skirmish in the car than she wanted to admit, so with flagging spirits she forced herself to go back downstairs.

Despite her apprehensions, the meal passed smoothly, with the conversational ball carried mainly by Lance and Matt as they discussed business. Jill found her attention wandering and failed to catch most of it. She was lost in nontherapeutic contemplation of the financial disaster Lucy had left, and wondering how things were progressing with Mr. Formby. She was expecting a letter from him sometime in the future. Not for the first time did she wish fervently she wasn't so dependent on her uncle for immediate material support. Not that he minded, she was sure. But that need did nothing to ease the situation between Lance and herself. It only enhanced the picture he saw of her being a money-grubbing little leech, and she found that that realization made her feel desolate.

In this frame of mind she barely noticed when Lance excused himself and went back to the shop—and Yvonne. Jill didn't appreciate the image that popped into her mind of the two of them working snugly side by side in the office. To erase that irritating vision, she described her morning's accomplishments to Matt, ending with, "And tomorrow we're taking a boat out to the cove and I'm going to get my first taste of saltwater diving."

"Already?" Matt questioned skeptically. "That's a little unusual, Jill. Are you ready for that?"

"It's only for a shallow dive, thirty feet at the most,

Scott says," Jill hastened to assure him. "He says I'm an excellent student, and I have confidence in myself. Don't worry, Uncle Matt. Nothing is going to happen."

The following morning, a typically reticent and reluctant Lance again transported her to the shop. In view of her uncle's reaction to her announcement, she didn't want to reveal Scott's plans to Lance, either. She knew he'd feel no hesitation in squelching their progress, and she was so excited at the prospect of actually swimming and diving in the Atlantic, she didn't want to give him the chance. Besides, they would be in a calm-watered cove, not the open ocean. They'd be perfectly safe. Scott was a highly experienced diver.

She flew out of the car and into the shop, missing the brow-raised look with which Lance watched her. Scott was in the storeroom, organizing their neoprene suits and the other gear.

"Are you as excited as you look?" he greeted her, smiling appreciatively at the brilliance of her blue eyes.

"Do I look it?" she returned breathlessly. At his nod, she added, "Do you blame me?"

"No." He laughed, and gave her a playful slap on her rump. "Go and get into that cute suit of yours, and here"—he handed her the full-length diving suit that was now hers—"put this on, too." As she swung open the door to the ladies' locker room, she heard him call, "If you have any trouble, I'll be glad to come in and help."

She shook her head at his irrepressible flirtatiousness. Lance was right. Scott Dougherty was a good-time Charlie. He wasn't ready to settle down to a serious relationship. Of couse, neither was she, Jill told herself firmly, so they were the perfect companions for each other.

Scott had informed her previously that the full-length

wet suits were a must at that time of the year, for the water temperature was well below seventy degrees, the temperature at which a diver could comfortably enter the water without a suit. Even then, some divers wore half-suits or sleeveless shirts made of the same spongy substance.

Quickly she was into the suit and back in the storeroom, being fitted with the inflatable safety vest, a weight belt calibrated to her needs, and then the heavy compressed-air tanks. Carrying their fins, they went out the back entrance to a small dock where a flat-bottomed motorboat was moored. After tossing the fins in and then stepping into the boat themselves, Scott released the boat from its mooring rope and started the motor. They headed out from the shore at an angle that took them around a jutting piece of land and into a smallish cove where the water remained calm and stable.

"Okay, Jill," Scott said as he cut the motor and tossed the anchor over, "inflate the divers-down flag, and in we'll go."

Jill complied, eagerly readying the doughnut-shaped inner tube with its attached flag of orange-red with one diagonal white stripe. Scott would tow the flag with them as they dived, so passersby in other boats would know there were divers operating in the area.

Next they strapped on their fins; hers were smaller and shorter than Scott's. She knew this was because she had not yet developed leg muscles strong enough to be able to control the longer, stiffer-bladed ones Scott was wearing. Being an experienced diver, he could wear the larger fins, which generated greater thrust through the water, without getting leg cramps.

"All right, now," he said after dropping the diver's flag over the side. "I'll enter first, then you. We'll use the stride entrance." His concerned green-brown eyes latched onto the face of his pupil. "Scared?"

"No," Jill returned calmly, meeting his gaze steadily. Surprisingly, she was not, even though this was her first dive in the salty ocean. They had practiced for the past two days in the sanctuary of the heated pool, and she knew swimming in the colder salt water would be an entirely different experience, but she felt equal to the challenge.

"That's my girl. Well, here goes." And with that he placed the regulator mouthpiece between his teeth and entered the water. After he broke the surface to give her the go-ahead, she copied his example, holding her mask in position over her face by pressing the fingers of one hand firmly on the lens, spread so she could see between them. Then she strode out over the water from the side of the boat as if she were on dry land.

Instantly she felt the fins hit the water. She kicked her legs together and forced her arms down through the water to her waist. These motions brought her descent into the water to a halt, and just her head was above the surface.

Scott, treading water nearby, gave her the forefinger-to-thumb sign of approval, then the thumbs-down signal for descent. Together they upended and began heading toward the bottom, roughly thirty feet below.

Chapter Seven

As they descended, the first thing that struck Jill was the feeling of isolation the sudden silence below the surface caused. Their bubbles shimmered upward past their face masks as they finned downward. Scott had warned Jill that the bottom in the cove would not be as interesting as it would be at greater depths farther out in the ocean, but this was just her initiation to saltwater diving, not a sightseeing trip.

As they swam side by side, Jill equalized the pressure in her mask by breathing into it through her nose.

Shortly they reached the sandy bottom, which was swept by ocean currents into ripples and hillocks. The long tentacles of seaweed waved to and fro, reminding Jill of the movement of prairie grass in the wind back on the Kansas plains. Even though Scott had warned her of the mundane appearance, she was thrilled. Familiarity may have bred contempt in Scott, but it was all brand new and intriguing to Jill. Breathing calmly and regularly from her compressed-air tanks, which were lighter on her back now that she was submerged, Jill journeyed off on a small exploratory swim. She assumed Scott was behind her, and it was only after she had spotted a school of fish, silvery gray in color with two prominent yellow lines running the length of their bodies, milling aimlessly about, that she turned, intending to point them out to Scott, and noticed he was not there.

Remembering his stern counsel about staying together, she began threading herself through the long slick seaweed streamers to retrace what she hoped was the way she'd swum in search of him. Finally she saw him. He was poised in one spot, fiddling with his regulator; then he caught sight of her and beckoned her over. As she swam toward him, she saw him make the "cutthroat" gesture, meaning his air supply was cut off. He pointed to his mouthpiece, then to his mouth. Recalling how he'd teased about pretending to need to buddybreathe with her on their first dive, she was undisturbed by his action. She came to a halt several feet away, eyeing him good-naturedly through her mask.

Scott removed his regulator mouthpiece, showing it to her. Still she failed to act, and he headed toward her, his regulator completely abandoned and resting on his chest. As he neared her, she saw for the first time the genuinely anxious look to his eyes behind the lens of his mask.

Reaching out, he touched her mouthpiece, and she obediently opened her mouth, gently pulled the mouthpiece from between her teeth, and handed it to him. His chest rose fractionally as he took a lungful of the compressed air.

He hadn't been fooling! He was truly in danger! She

suddenly felt terrible for having doubted him and causing him such anxiety.

Handing the regulator back to her, he gave the thumbs-up sign for ascent. Together they rose to the surface, sharing the regulator's life-giving supply of air, and broke the surface beside the divers-down flag. Grasping the side of the float, they supported themselves as they breathed now from the open air above the water.

"Scott! What happened?" Jill asked, round-eyed. "I thought you were teasing."

"Jill, honey," he got out between ragged breaths, "no one teases when they're on a dive. It's serious business beneath the waves, and . . . " He paused to fill his lungs again with a gulp. "Even I abandon my devil-may-care attitude down there. I could see what you were thinking. That's why I almost had to take the blasted regulator right out of your mouth."

"Oh, I'm so sorry, Scott," was all she could mumble as a wave of chagrin overtook her.

"And another thing," he added, looking more than a little disturbed with her now, "don't ever swim off on your own. Always make sure your diving partner is in sight. Understand?"

"Yes, Scott," Jill answered meekly. She forbore to mention she'd merely assumed he'd be following her. She realized now with a stab of guilt that one never assumed anything under the water.

She felt thoroughly chastened and a little frightened as she followed Scott to the motorboat, where he helped haul her in, pulling the flag float after them. Scott could literally have passed out and died down there if she hadn't returned when she did.

The mood was somber as Scott started up the boat

and headed back to the dive shop's dock. Jill had never felt so awful in her life, and it showed on her frightened face. She was too petrified to question him about what had happened to his regulator. That would be explained later, when they'd both calmed down.

After he'd secured the boat to its moorings and was preparing to help Jill out, Scott glimpsed the horrified little face of his companion.

"Aw, Jill," he said, drawing her into his arms, "it's all right. I'm alive."

All this served to do was break the dam of tears gathering behind her eyelids, and she let loose with a torrent of humiliated tears.

"Hey, now! Stop this!" Scott ordered, lifting her chin to bestow a consoling kiss on her trembling lips.

"I'm sorry, Scott. That seems to be all I can say," she said jaggedly as she allowed him to assist her from the boat.

Gathering their fins and the deflated diving flag and inner tube, Scott urged her back up to the shop.

"It's okay, honey. Believe me, I could have ascended directly to the surface by holding my breath. I'm an experienced diver, and thirty feet or so would have been no hardship, but I was worried about you, since I couldn't spot you in the midst of all that seaweed and I'd exhausted my supply in my lungs waiting for you to reappear. You learned an important lesson today— the hard way."

"I'll say I learned it the hard way," Jill agreed sadly as they entered the back door of the shop.

"What did you learn the hard way?" Lance's voice had an acid bite to it. He stood at the side of the plate-glass window with a look on his face that would have rivaled the Medusa's.

Jill started, not having been aware of his presence, and looked at his angry face in consternation.

"You go on and change. I'll explain," Scott murmured in her ear.

Jill was only too happy to comply, and hurried through the dressing-room door as she heard Scott's quiet voice begin a matter-of-fact recital of the incident.

What she didn't hear was Lance's reaction, but after she was changed and was coming back to the shop, the dressing-room door swung open and Scott stepped through. Jill stopped short, catching sight of his flushed and furious-looking face.

"What's the matter?"

"Captain Bligh can tell you," Scott returned shortly, and brushed past her in an uncharacteristic manner to enter the storeroom door.

Jill followed him in, wanting to give him her diving suit.

He took it from her and muttered, "You'd better get going. *He's* waiting."

"Yes," Jill said in a soft, confused little voice. She was disturbed by his behavior and wondered what she should do.

Scott looked up at her sharply. "Don't keep *him* waiting."

With a mental shrug, Jill turned and entered the dive shop. Lance stood, hands in his pockets, legs spread in an aggressive stance, staring out at the ocean, which was more placid today than the atmosphere of the room. The air fairly crackled with tension. Jill swallowed convulsively, wishing she didn't have to rely on him to return her to the Lane house.

As if he had a sixth sense that warned him she was in

the room, Lance turned, but his face gave nothing away. The gray eyes were shuttered, the mouth uncommunicative, even on the drive home. Not for anything was Jill going to be the first to break that oppressive silence.

At the house, she expected him to drive off, but instead, he drove around to the back after she had gotten out.

Like an animal scurrying to its burrow when scenting danger, Jill fled up the stairs and along the corridor to her uncle's room. There was no answer to her light tap, and a peek in the door found him sound asleep, spread across his bed fully clothed. As she stood at the side of his bed, watching that aged chest rise and fall in deep slumberous breathing, she felt a surge of love well up in her heart. He was such a dear man, and she loved him more than she could remember loving anyone but her mother.

With a sigh she turned and tiptoed from the room, closing the door softly. She turned, preparing to go to her own room, and stopped, gasping in surprise. Lance stood just inches away, seeming to have materialized out of the woodwork.

"Is he asleep?" he asked with an ominously quiet voice.

"Yes." Jill regarded him with wary eyes.

Without a word, Lance whirled and headed for the stairs, disappearing down them rapidly. Jill took a deep breath, realizing she hadn't been breathing while he stood there, then darted into her room to wait for dinner. She wasn't going to chance running into him before the evening meal. Grabbing a diving manual, she flopped on her bed and did some studying to while away some of the afternoon before she showered and changed.

Later, after she was dressed in a soft clingy dress of a pale mauve shade, which gave her a boost of confidence, she slowly descended the stairs, steeling herself for the unavoidable exposure to Lance. Had he had a chance to speak to Uncle Matt? What repercussions should she expect from the morning's misadventure? What had been the trouble with Scott's regulator? These questions concerned her as she made the trip to the first floor.

To her immense relief she found only her uncle in the library, sipping what looked like a martini.

"Are you supposed to drink alcohol, Uncle Matt?" she asked without preliminaries. It was something she'd wondered about previously but had not had the chance to ask about.

Matt chuckled as he received her kiss on the cheek. "Yes, my dear. In moderation. Actually, I allow myself only one a day. Lance hasn't come in yet, so I'll be your bartender this evening. What would you like?"

Jill was startled. She hadn't heard Lance leave again, but he must have after being thwarted in his attempt to see Matt when he wanted to. Feeling like a criminal granted a reprieve, she smiled brightly at her uncle and said, "Just a small glass of sherry, please, Uncle Matt." She wanted to keep a clear head for the inevitable showdown.

As Matt poured her sherry, the sound of a powerful car could be heard driving up outside, then passing on to the back. It was Lance, of course. Jill felt her stomach doing flip-flops as she waited for him to put in an appearance. If Matt noticed her preoccupation, he didn't reveal it as he questioned her.

"I had an unusually long nap today, so I missed seeing you this noon. How did it go?"

Jill was prevented from answering as Lance's clipped

response sounded from the door. He'd come in through the kitchen and had approached silently.

"That's exactly what I want to talk to you about, Matt."

Both pairs of blue eyes jerked in surprise to view the man standing just inside the room.

"Oh?" Matt Lane's voice sounded worried in reaction to the serious tone in Lance's. His troubled eyes shifted to Jill. "Did you have any difficulties?"

Again Lance's intervention hindered Jill from speaking for herself. She was getting extremely irritated with him.

"Dougherty's regulator malfunctioned today, cutting off his air supply. They had to share Jill's to return to the surface." Lance's digestion of the details in an accusing manner had the effect of causing Matt to sit down abruptly in a nearby chair.

"But, how—?" he began.

"Dougherty apparently failed to give it the thorough inspection it deserved, and that, coupled with his student's swimming off by herself, almost cost a life." Lance's voice was cold, and his flinty eyes impaled Jill where she sat.

Her throat worked convulsively but she was unable to make a defense. Terrible though he made it sound, she knew it was the truth. Her uncle was rendered equally speechless as his dazed eyes shifted from Lance to Jill.

Lance, naturally, had plenty to say.

"It seems to me Dougherty's judgment is a little clouded where Miss Taggert is concerned. It was too early in her instruction for her to be taken out on a dive."

"Then you don't think Scott is the proper instructor

for Jill?" her uncle questioned slowly, fixing Lance with earnest eyes.

"I do not!"

"Then you take over, Lance."

Lance and Jill simultaneously opened their mouths to object, but Matt rose agitatedly to replace his glass on the bartop, saying, "I wanted you to teach her in the first place. Now this just proves my gut feelings were correct." His voice had hardened with resolve, and as he swung to face them, they could see his mind was made up. There would be no appeal. But Jill had to try.

"Uncle Matt, perhaps I should suspend taking instruction for the present. Besides, Lance is much too busy. He's—"

Her uncle stopped her with a wave of his hand. "We've been through all that. He'll make time. Mrs. Flemming is perfectly capable of running the office alone." He cast disapproving eyes that held a private message to Lance. There was some sort of undercurrent there Jill couldn't comprehend, but she could see Lance had already acceded to Matt's wishes. It was written on his face, along with dismay that he had been maneuvered into this situation. His eyes met hers across the room, and they almost seemed to say: See what you've done?

John came shuffling in to announce dinner, and silently the three of them followed his stooped form into the dining room, each engrossed in his own thoughts.

As soon as it was possible, Jill pleaded exhaustion and escaped to her room, turning down dessert and coffee. As she hung up her dress she thought ruefully that she was becoming a recluse in the lilac splendor of her room. It would never do, but somehow she had to marshal her thoughts about the prospect of having Lance become her new teacher. The very idea was frightening. She decided she was going to have to dredge up courage she never used before, because she had no intention of giving up lessons completely. There was more at stake than just learning to dive. She wanted to become a qualified instructor herself; then, when Scott left, she could take his place and become an asset to her uncle rather than a liability. Perhaps she would be able to repay some of the money her step-mother had extorted—although ten thousand dollars was an awesome amount. It was in a totally unrestful state that she was able to get to sleep that night.

The following morning at breakfast, which Jill took with her uncle and Lance out on the side porch, she got an indication of just what working with Lance was going to be like.

"When you get through there, we can leave," Lance said, his voice even, as he buried himself behind a newspaper.

"Leave?" Jill questioned, staring at the raised news-paper as if she could see through it to the man behind.

The paper was lowered, and Lance regarded her blandly. "Yes. For the shop. For your lessons."

"But it's Sunday."

"How very astute of you. Yes, it's Sunday, and as you pointed out, I'm a busy man. The shop is closed today, therefore I have plenty of time to instruct you." He didn't say "in diving," and Jill had the feeling he wasn't talking about just that, either.

Her uncle, who had been watching this interchange, spoke. "Surely, there's no need to start today."

"On the contrary," Lance said. Miss Tag . . . *Jill* has expressed a desire to waste no time in learning all she can. In view of what happened yesterday, I feel it's a good idea she return to saltwater practice immediately."

"You're taking me out on a dive?" Jill broke in, staring at him in astonishment.

"Not exactly. I'm going to test you on the beach."

"Why not the pool?"

"The pool is for sissies."

They engaged in a battle of the eyes, both of them determined to show the other that they weren't in the least affected by the situation.

"I don't know. It seems so irregular," Matt remarked in a puzzled voice.

"Your niece is irregular," Lance observed dryly, and rose, folding the paper and tucking it under his arm. "Well . . . Jill?" His gray eyes held hers a moment; then she, too, stood up.

"Ready whenever you are," she said softly, but in a voice that illustrated she knew what game he was playing, and although she might dislike the rules, was ready to play it too.

Fifteen minutes later they were on their way. Jill was so used to the silent car trips, she was even coming to enjoy them. At least with him she wasn't forced to carry on sparkly conversation, she reflected wryly as she watched the pines and palms slide by.

No one was at the shop today, and after Lance unlocked the door, then relocked it behind them, they both retreated to their respective locker rooms to change. Jill met him in the supply room, where she got a second taste of how different things were going to be.

"How much do you know about the proper care and storage of your diving equipment?" he asked, his manner completely objective and businesslike.

"Well, after diving in salt water, you should rinse the neoprene suits in fresh water."

Lance nodded. "And then what?"

"Once they're dry, dust them with pure talc and store in a cool, dry place away from light."

"Good. How about putting oil on the zippers?"

She smiled inwardly at his attempt to trip her up. He really did think she was stupid. "Never!" she replied adamantly. "Use only silicone lubricant."

"Very good, Miss Taggert. You get an A+. From now on you personally will care for your own suit." He turned to a locker and opened it. "This is your very own locker. Keep your suit in it, along with your other things. Here is your key." He tossed it to her. "You will be responsible for it. Dougherty isn't going to be here to coddle you anymore. Now, suit up. I want to see how much you know."

With that slightly double-edged remark hanging between them, they both proceeded to don suits, air tanks, weight belts, vests, and regulators. Jill noted something different about the regulators this time. They were double ones, with two hoses leading to two separate mouthpieces, thereby offering two different channels for obtaining air.

Lance caught the curious look with which she was studying them. "It's called an octopus regulator," he explained patiently, but with an undercurrent of grimness. "If you both had been wearing them the other day, Scott would have been in no danger. It was a serious breach of policy for you not be outfitted in them. Which just proves my point about his judgment being clouded where you're concerned."

"Do I just let the extra hang free?"

Lance nodded, handed her her fins, and walked out of the room, through the shop, to the glass door.

Jill followed him down to the beach, where the waves

were rolling in, foaming over the golden sand. He turned to her.

"Put on your fins and prepare to enter the water."

In silence Jill obeyed, pulling the straps up behind her ankles, then walked backward into the water until it came up to her waist. Lance did the same, coming to a halt beside her.

"All right, Miss Taggert. Demonstrate your drown-proofing technique," he demanded coolly.

Without a word Jill swam out to water that was over her head and went into a dead man's float. Submerged, hanging vertically in the water with her face below the surface, she hung her legs and arms down limply. This she had learned was called the resting position.

The object of drown-proofing was to allow an exhausted diver, far out to sea, to float for long periods of time until rescued. Next, Jill got ready to take a breath. Slowly raising her arms at her sides to just under the surface, she spread her legs in preparation to kick. Out of the corner of her eye she could see Lance observing her from a point at some distance underwater. Bringing her arms down at the same time that she kicked, she propelled herself so her mouth just broke the surface, exhaling prior to that moment. She inhaled a breath through her mouth, then dropped back to the resting position. She knew she had inhaled just the right amount of air, because neither did she have difficulty sinking, nor did she fall too deeply below the surface. A quick glance at Lance revealed he was satisfied with her display, for he gave the thumbs-up signal to rise, and together they broke the surface, several feet apart from each other.

His only words of praise consisted of: "That's fine. Now, I'm a panicked, exhausted diver; rescue me."

With that, he sank, floundering like someone in need of help.

Instantly Jill was at his side, reaching toward the capsule of compressed gas which was contained in his inflatable safety vest. After she started the vest inflating, she began towing Lance's deadweight to the surface. It was hard, but not impossible, and she received no help from him. He was making it as difficult for her as possible, she knew, and that made her all the more determined to be successful at this rescue attempt.

As they broke the surface, instinctively she knew Lance's greater bulk and weight would make the towing technique of holding his head between her palms while she kicked backward on her back out of the question. Instead she made sure his face was well clear of the water, removed his mask to give him more air, and performing the sidestroke with one arm, she grasped the collar of his safety vest, towing him behind her. It was rough going, but after they had progressed approximately fifty feet and she knew the water was waist-deep again, Jill stood up, maintaining her support of Lance's limp body. As she did this, he immediately pulled from her grasp and stood up too, facing her.

"Well, well, Miss Taggert. You surprise me. I should say you astound me," he remarked in a sardonic voice.

Jill watched him through narrowed eyes. "And just why is that?" she asked suspiciously.

"Frankly, I didn't expect you to know anything."

"What did you think we were doing all this time?" Jill asked haughtily, and instantly regretted her question as Lance threw back his head and laughed furiously.

"What was I supposed to think? The only time I saw you two together was when Dougherty had you in the clinches. For all I know, you spent all your time making love." Jill's gasp of outrage failed to check his hateful voice. "That's probably how Dougherty slipped up yesterday. You had him so bewitched he couldn't see straight. That's how your type works—"

Jill couldn't bear to hear any more. With action propelled by hate, her hand lashed out and made stinging contact with his cheek, bringing to a finish his denigrating words. She only hoped that reddening skin hurt half as much as her palm did. How could anyone have a jaw so hard? Feeling dismay at her instinctive reaction to his insult, she watched the nerve jump in that rocklike jaw as Lance's arms snaked out to grasp her shoulders in a punishing grip.

"So you want to play rough, do you?" he grated through clenched teeth.

As she was wrenched against his body, her flipper-footed right leg tripped over the sea bottom, and she stumbled forward, the unexpected action propelling her against him, and they both tumbled, Lance falling backward into the water.

He maintained his vise grip on her slender shoulders, unwittingly pulling her below the surface before she was able to gulp in a fresh breath of sustaining air. Thrashing frantically, she struggled to rise and found herself floundering helplessly, her hands pushing impotently against Lance's chest, forcing him downward with the weight of his tanks completing the task.

It was entirely due to his supreme physical condition that he was able to shift out from under her and stand up, grasping Jill under the arms and unceremoniously hauling her up to stand unsteadily before him. She presented a pathetic picture, trembling, dripping salt water, and gasping for breath, taking in the sweet air in quick frenzied gulps.

Lance retained his steadying hold on her, providing

unwavering support. Weak and exhausted, Jill sagged against him. A hand tipped her chin upward, as Lance scrutinized her face. "Are you all right?"

Still too shaken to speak, Jill shook her head, her luminous eyes gazing into his in confusion. Had she mistakenly heard concern in his deep voice? As she watched, those compelling male lips descended, covering hers with a kiss as sweet as the air she'd filled her lungs with.

The pressure of his mouth increased with passion, drawing her into a whirlpool of feelings. The kiss was a raging sea, a tidal wave rising up to engulf her. The hands at her shoulders slipped down over her rib cage to slide around her waist, trapping her against his body in a suffocating embrace. But instead of being a frightening experience like before when she'd found herself breathlessly trapped underwater, it was glorious torture. His strong hands molded her hips more firmly against his, and his mouth became hard and demanding as hers blossomed under it.

Suddenly she found herself appalled at the intensity with which she was responding to him, and with one concerted effort she pushed mightily against his muscular chest, wedging a space between them wide enough to pull their locked lips apart.

Blue eyes shot rejection and disgust at flinty ones. Lance's arms dropped to his sides like leaden anchors, and he stepped back, widening the distance between them.

"That, Miss Taggert, is the end of lesson one," he stated unequivocally, and removing his fins with careless yanks, waded out of the water toward the beach.

Jill found her voice and protested, "But I haven't learned anything today."

Lance checked his steps, pivoting to cast her a glittering look. "Oh, I think you have," he drawled meaningfully, and strode up the beach to the shop without a backward glance.

Jill allowed herself a few moments to collect her scattered wits and pride; then, removing her fins, she waded out of the water to trudge back toward the shop. She ducked into the locker room to change, hoping Lance would be finished in the supply room by the time she was ready to go in. Filling a large basin in the locker room with cool tap water, she proceeded to soak her neoprene suit while she dressed in her dry jeans and T-shirt. Then she reluctantly walked into the supply room, only to find Lance there.

Wordlessly they placed their suits on wooden hangers and locked away their masks, fins, and regulators. Finally she knew she had to ask: "How can I dust my suit with talc if it's not dry?" and hated doing so.

Lance carefully avoided looking at her as he replied, "Tomorrow, prior to putting it on again. The talc also acts as an aid to putting the suit on easily."

"Oh, yes, of course." She stood irresolute, not knowing whether to go or stay.

Lance turned out the light and led the way to the car, apparently sure she would follow. She did, of course, her steps dragging.

He didn't immediately start the car, but sat, his long fingers lightly drumming the steering wheel, and stared in front of him. Jill fidgeted nervously, waiting.

"Miss Taggert," he began heavily, and Jill wondered why he always used the formal appellation when they were alone. Perhaps as a device to keep her at a distance? "Tomorrow we will begin your instruction— officially. As soon as we arrive in the mornings, we will suit up and proceed to the beach. When we are through, you will drive yourself back to the house." Jill's face showed her surprise, and he added, "Mrs. Flemming can bring me home at the end of the day."

And with no further word he started the car and drove out of the lot toward the highway.

The remainder of the day was spent reading the paper and playing chess. It was Consuelo's day off, and Jill and Matt cooked up a concoction using various leftovers. Matt's idea of what to throw in the pan bordered on the absurd, and they had a great time laughing and arguing. But when it was all done, even Lance had to begrudgingly admit their dinner, which they dubbed "Matt's Frying Pan Flambé," wasn't half-bad.

Jill had no idea what Lance told her uncle about their abortive session, but it seemed to have sufficed, for he asked no questions of her.

It was a more restful night for Jill than the previous one, helped somewhat by her avowal not to let Lance get under her skin. She would be the best student his criticizing eyes had ever beheld. He would find no fault with her.

Monday morning there was no patronizing, only the calm instruction of a student by a teacher. Lance told her a few things Scott hadn't gotten around to.

As they stood down on the beach preparing to enter the water, Lance asked, "What do you know about nitrogen narcosis?"

"Nitrogen narcosis?" Jill repeated vaguely. The term meant nothing to her. She shook her head. "I don't believe I'm familiar with it."

"Sometimes it's called 'rapture of the deep.' Put your fins on," he added, then continued explaining the term as he began wading backward into the water. "It occurs at depths of two hundred feet or more when nitrogen accumulates in a diver's system, causing him to experience strange 'raptures' or a kind of intoxication. Cousteau discovered the cause for it. One of his divers abandoned his mouthpiece at three hundred and ninety-six feet, thinking he could breathe underwater without the aid of tanks; of course he was wrong."

"He drowned?" Jill guessed, horrified.

Lance nodded grimly. "Of course the likelihood of your doing much diving at that depth is remote, but every diver should be aware of the rapture. Now," he said briskly, "today I want to also make sure you know about the offshore currents—how to react to them, even using them to your advantage."

For the rest of the morning, and on until Wednesday, he made her retrace some of the steps Scott had already covered, until he was satisfied she really was ready for a dive.

Scott was not in evidence, and Jill learned from Yvonne that he was taking a week's vacation down in Miami and Ft. Lauderdale. Jill wondered if it might have been at Lance's direction.

Matt came by on Friday to observe the lessons, John having driven him in the second car and waited to take her home. Jill had grown to enjoy driving the Mercedes, but she was secretly pleased Lance wouldn't have Yvonne for a chauffeur. She'd noticed that their good-byes, when they finally did drive up to the house at the end of the day, were longer than seemed necessary.

By the following Monday, when Jill had been with her uncle two weeks, she was beginning to feel she'd always lived there. It seemed so natural to wake up in the lilac-decorated room, so natural to greet her uncle every morning with a kiss. Even driving with Lance to the shop now had a regularity that seemed normal. She wondered if he'd ever unbend enough to converse with her as if they were ordinary people. Probably not. She also wondered if he'd heard from the investigators he'd said he was going to hire. Perhaps he had changed his mind, especially in view of her uncle's patent acceptance of her as his once-thought-dead niece.

Breaking into her reverie, Lance said in warning tones, "Scott Dougherty will be back at the shop this morning. I suggest you remember what I said about him."

Her immediate inclination was to tell him to mind his own business, but judging from their past altercations, she knew it would only make him more stubborn.

"Yes, Mr. Darrel," she replied so meekly he threw a suspicious look at her.

He looked like he was about to say something, then thought better of it and returned his concentration to steering the Mercedes into the parking lot.

Chapter Eight

If Jill had thought relations between Scott and herself would be stilted, she hadn't reckoned with his affable nature. Also, perhaps he was relaxed after his vacation, for as soon as she entered the shop he was there, greeting her as if nothing had ever happened.

"Hello, Jill. How are you?" His prosaic words were accompanied by a thorough scrutiny of her surprised face.

"Fine, Scott," she returned a little breathlessly, remembering Lance's warning. She was acutely aware of his presence directly behind her. "I . . . I have to get ready for my lesson," she added lamely, and began to move toward the dressing-room door.

Scott apparently knew what the score was, for he simply nodded and let her go. She was followed by the tall form of her new instructor, who, as soon as the dressing-room door closed behind them, remarked in a return to his baiting manner, "Very nice, Miss Taggert. That should put him off the scent."

Jill whirled to face her tormentor like an angry badger backed into a corner.

"Mr. Darrel! If you will concern yourself only with being my instructor and not playing dog in the manger, we will get along famously."

Her abrupt lunge into the locker room caused her to miss the uplift of his arched brows and the astonished look on his face.

Minutes later, when she joined him to don the diving suit and equipment, he astounded her by saying, "Matt will be dropping by in a few minutes to accompany us out in the boat."

"Out in the boat?"

"That's what I said. I think we'll see if your return to the cove will be an improvement over last time."

"But he didn't say anything about that at breakfast," Jill protested, still hardly believing her ears.

"I just called him. John's bringing him along now."

Jill momentarily stopped strapping on her weight belt to stare at him.

"Come on, Miss Taggert. Get ready," he instructed her complacently, and since he was all through, left the room, heading for the shop.

Hurriedly she finished, snatched up her fins, and followed him, arriving in the shop just as Matt stepped through the door.

"Well, Jill," he boomed in an immensely pleased voice. "So Lance thinks you're ready for a dive. Good! Good!" He clapped his hands together appreciatively, and directed his next words to Lance, who just then came out of the office with a slightly disgruntled-looking Yvonne on his trail. "Are we ready?"

Lance nodded, turned to Yvonne and said, "We'll be

back in less than an hour; I'll return the salesman's call then," and led the way out to the motorboat.

This time there were no hitches. Lance steered the boat into the sheltered cove, tossed over the anchor and the diver's flag, then preceded Jill into the water. Together they descended, swimming toward the bottom in perfect unison.

Whereas Jill's suit was a deep blue, Lance's suit was completely black, and somehow Jill felt it appropriate. The somber color, combined with the way the spongy neoprene fitted smoothly over his muscular frame, made him appear almost sinister. But he swam with firm, determined kicks, cutting through the water with an assurance that gave her a feeling of security. She kept him firmly in sight, and he her.

They reached the bottom simultaneously, and Lance signaled to her the direction they should go, leading the way.

The water was a clear blue at that depth, and as Jill finned after Lance, she was able to see the rocklike formation that marked the beginning of the reef. The mask with its perimeter of black rubber gave her the feeling of having tunnel vision, making her wish she could see clearly without it. Scott had told her that some divers wore special contact lenses, eliminating the feeling that something could sneak up on them from the side before their limited peripheral vision spotted it. This fear kept her looking from side to side, but the only forms of life were schools of fish.

Lance had stopped before an outcropping of coral, some of it shaped like antlers, some like the convolutions of the human brain. There were coatings of sponge covering some of the boulders. He was pointing down near a crevice where an ugly oval-shaped head glared back at them balefully, then retreated within its hideout. Jill recognized it as one of the eel family, and abruptly stopped, refusing to come any nearer to the inhospitable member of the denizens of the deep, thus drawing an amused look from her instructor. He swam on, pointing out various things that were of interest, including some rose-red-colored fish Jill recognized as snappers, the same silver-gray ones she'd seen on her first dive, plus seemingly hundreds more. The fish didn't seem to mind the intrusion of the human swimmers into their domain, even coming closer for a personal look of their own.

Once, near the bottom, its wide graceful batlike fins propelling it wraithlike over the sand, a sting ray was sighted. Jill judiciously watched it from a distance, admiring the smoothness with which it swam in search of food.

The time passed too quickly for her before Lance was signaling her to ascend. Once again they kicked side by side to the surface. Matt was there to help Jill aboard, while Lance agilely heaved himself into the boat.

"Well, how was it?" Matt asked, once they were on their way.

"Wonderful," Jill replied.

The wind was whipping her dampened hair about her face, and her eyes were sparkling from excitement. Underwater, where neither could speak, she and Lance had been forced to be a team, to work for their mutual benefit. She'd found she'd liked that.

Matt turned to Lance. "How did she do?" he shouted over the sound of the engine.

Lance seemed to consider it for a moment. Jill held her breath, wondering what he would say. Finally he spoke, seemingly against his will.

"Your niece is a good student. She has the potential to be a good diver, even an excellent one. She's levelheaded, a strong swimmer. You have no worries." After this surprising admission, he gave himself completely over to steering the boat back to the dock.

Matt leaned over to give Jill's shoulder a squeeze. "That's my girl," he said proudly.

Jill was dumbfounded. That Lance would actually make public commendation was beyond her wildest hopes. She regarded his broad back wonderingly.

It was as if she was in a trance when they'd docked and Matt escorted her up to the shop. Fleetingly her eyes had met with Lance's, and just for a moment those inscrutable gray eyes seemed open and communicative. What she had seen there puzzled her. Could it be he was beginning to change his opinion of her?

Scott met them at the door, his expression appearing anxious, but Matt's first words cleared it.

"She did just fine, Lance said. They had a good dive."

"That's great, Jill," Scott said, drawing her aside. "Say," he added, after Lance had passed out of earshot, "have dinner with me tonight?"

"Oh, Scott, I . . . " Jill was nonplussed. What should she do? Lance would become difficult if she accepted. But then, who was he to tell her what to do? In a rush of resurfacing antagonism, she agreed. "I'd love to. What time?"

"I'll pick you up at six. Wear something pretty." With that, he went off to attend to some customers who'd just arrived.

Matt was in the office, and Jill hurried into the locker room to change. Lance had already rinsed and hung up his wet suit, she noted, when she took her rinsed one into the supply room. Hopefully, he was still in the men's locker room, and she might be able to escape before seeing him again.

Feeling somewhat like a fugitive from the law, she rejoined her uncle and John, who'd been having a cup of coffee with the secretary in the office, and together they returned to the house for lunch.

When she informed Matt about her dinner date, he exhibited none of the anxiety Lance had implied he would.

"Why, that's just fine, sweetheart. Do you good to get out with some young man instead of spending your free hours with an old man like me." Beaming blue eyes bestowed approval on her.

"Don't say things like that, Uncle Matt," Jill reproved sternly, rising from her chair at the side of the dining table to wrap her arm around her uncle's shoulder. "I love you, and I love being with you. If you didn't want me to go, I wouldn't. But I really didn't have a good reason for refusing Scott."

Her uncle's wrinkled old hand patted her ivory-smooth one. "And I'm glad you didn't. I'd like to see you get out more. See some sights." He pushed his chair back, and together they walked out to the hall, his steps slightly leaden. "I guess all the excitement this morning was a bit wearing, my dear, and I'm going to have to lie down for a while."

He cast apologetic eyes to his niece, who answered, "I think I'll go explore outside. Take a walk to the beach, perhaps."

"Good," Matt approved, and slowly made his way up the stairs as Jill watched his progress until he disappeared at the top.

Outside, she decided to follow the path behind the house down to the beach. The sky was a brilliant blue, deep purple at its zenith, and she could hear the soft washing of the waves on the shore getting louder as she approached. The path ran through tall, gently waving stalks of grasses, then ended in the golden sand.

Choosing a spot near the shore, Jill sank down to watch the waves and the seagulls wheeling overhead, filling the air with their strident call.

Staring at the surf, Jill was reminded of the first day she and Lance had gone to the shop to begin her instructions with him as her new teacher. She felt heat in her cheeks as she remembered that devastating kiss and her own shameful abandonment to it. Why had he done it? It seemed so incongruous for a man who appeared to dislike and mistrust her to kiss her in that way. A slow curling sensation began in the pit of her stomach, and Jill rose in agitation, deciding the isolation afforded by sitting alone on the beach was too conducive to thoughts of Lance. Turning reluctantly, she wandered back to the house.

The mail was delivered to the rural mailbox on the highway, and whoever had the time, John or Consuelo, went out to retrieve it. It was placed on a marble-topped table in the hall, separated into piles for Lance and Matt. Jill had absently noted this during her time there, and today, as she entered the house, out of the corner of her eye she spied an envelope apart from the others. She glanced down as she made to go past, and her step was arrested by the single letter. It was for her. Mr. Formby's return address revealed the identity of the sender, and Jill quickly tore the envelope open.

The auction had been completed and Mr. Formby awaited her instructions as to what to do with the few things remaining for her. Did she want them shipped to her or stored?

Jill realized in consternation that she really didn't know. Her life at present had so many untied strings.

How long would she be staying with Uncle Matt? The thought of ever having to leave weighed heavily on her heart. Obviously, at this juncture, the logical thing to do was have the items placed in storage, which would probably cost more in the long run than they were worth. But some of the things belonging to her mother, old photographs of long-dead relatives, a broken railroad watch belonging to her grandfather, and other items kept for the sake of nostalgia, were worth the expense to Jill. Which meant all the more that she'd better get going on learning to be a diving instructor if she ever had any hopes of earning money of her own.

Matt rose shortly after three, and the two of them played chess out on the side porch until it was time for her to go get ready for her evening out. Shortly before Scott was due to arrive, she returned downstairs to join her uncle in the library. Thankfully, Lance was late coming home and she hoped desperately she would be gone before he did.

"My, don't you look beautiful," her uncle said as she entered.

She had taken special care with her appearance, and had on a dress that emphasized the blue of her eyes and the darkness of her sleek black cap of hair. It was red, with a ruffled bodice, tied by two bows at the shoulders. The waist was softly gathered with a sash that showed off her narrow waist and gently curving hips to the best advantage. White flowers with pale blue accents patterned the vivid red background, giving the dress a bright tropical look.

Scott's approval was very evident when he arrived a few minutes later, his green-brown eyes dancing over her figure.

"Mmmm, I can see I'll have to stake my claim tonight if I want to have you all to myself. You're delectable," he observed as he helped her into his car, which was a slightly disreputable-looking green MG. Somehow Jill had expected something a little more stylish from the elegant Scott Dougherty.

"Where are we going?" she asked as he started the little sports car and began heading down the drive.

"To someplace special. You'll see. Do you like seafood?" He threw an inquiring look at her.

"I did, but after seeing so many fish today, I don't know if I have the heart to eat them now," Jill returned with a giggle that was choked off as the Mercedes turned into the drive just as they were prepared to exit it.

Lance's glowering face swiveled in surprise as they passed, Scott throwing a careless wave, Jill slinking down in her seat with a feeling of doom.

Darn! Why did he have to arrive just then? Why couldn't they have made their escape before he did? Would he be waiting for her when they returned later that night? This thought produced a strange mixture of fear and exhilaration in her that startled her. Scott was speaking, wrenching her back from fearful contemplation of the evening's end.

"Seriously, do you?"

"What?" Jill gazed at him in confusion.

"Like seafood?" Scott was looking at her strangely, as if she was a particularly dull child.

"Yes," she answered simply, and exerted herself to keep her mind on her companion and his conversation for the remainder of the drive.

The restaurant was situated in a marina, and they were ushered to a porch, partially enclosed, where they could view the various vessels of many different sizes and shapes bobbing at anchor. The sun slanted golden rays over the diners and a soft salty breeze ruffled the edges of the crisp white tablecloths. In the relaxed atmosphere, with the sound of water lapping docks mingling with the tinkle of ice in glasses and silverware scraping china, Jill was able to put all thought of Lance from her mind.

Scott was an excellent host, ordering the meal and wine with suave aplomb. Jill felt cosseted and contented. As they were eating the huge breaded butterfly shrimp and *coquilles St. Jacques,* excellently prepared, Scott began explaining about his activities when he'd been away.

"So I went to the library at Florida State University where there are maps to use for finding treasure kept on file. I was able to read up on a particularly interesting and fairly local disaster at sea, where a fleet of Spanish galleons on a mission to procure riches from the West Indies foundered in shallow water off the coast of Florida in 1715. The fleet was rumored to have been carrying fourteen million dollars in treasure."

"Really? Where did it go down?"

"Near Sebastian inlet, south of Cape Canaveral. For years there were rumors of beachcombers finding Spanish pieces of eight washed up on the beach, sometimes buried in the sand and found by metal-detecting devices."

"But the wrecked ships were never found?"

"Oh, yes, in the late fifties and early sixties, one intrepid individual organized a massive and expensive salvage operation and managed to find the site of the wreck, bringing up thousands of dollars' worth of silver and gold ingots, jewelry, coins, and even some Kiangsi Chinese porcelain."

"So what's left to look for?" Jill queried, pushing aside her plate, feeling satisfied and replete.

"There may be more or not; at any rate, diving in the wreck area appeals to me, and I'm planning on doing it tomorrow afternoon, since I don't have any students then."

Jill's interest was instantly secured. "Tomorrow, Scott?" She leaned forward, her eyes alight with enthusiasm. "Oh, do you think I could go with you?"

The blond man looked temporarily dubious, then shrugged. "Sure you can. There are a few of us, two besides me, and I don't see why it wouldn't be all right. There's safety in numbers. Be ready around noon, with your gear, and we'll leave directly from the shop. Have Matt's cook prepare you a packed lunch, a light one."

"Oh, Scott, I'm so excited," Jill said with a tremor in her voice and a gleam in her eye.

"Now, hold on," Scott cautioned. "There's not a great chance of finding anything. Especially since visibility in that area is not usually good—ten feet, on the average."

"Oh," Jill said, momentarily squelched; then her natural optimism reasserted itself. "That's all right. It should be a new and interesting experience at the least."

"That's true. Now, what would you like for dessert?" he asked, bringing the subject to a close.

"Nothing. I'm not big on sweets," Jill replied artlessly.

"That explains those gorgeous curves," her escort remarked softly as his eyes took them in appreciatively. "Well, if that's all you want, we'll go."

They rose and left the porch, which was now bathed in the pale rosy glow of the setting sun. Jill couldn't believe it was already nearing eight-thirty when she saw the time on an antique clock in the entrance. Scott took

117

her down to walk along the pier and look at the yachts tugging gently at their mooring ropes as if they were eager to be out to sea. Some of the craft were huge, costing more money that Jill could imagine.

By the time they returned to the little green car, it was fully dark.

"Would you like to go somewhere else?" Scott inquired before starting the engine.

Jill was delightfully exhausted, filled with good food, good wine, and reclining her head back on the top of the bucket seat, she rolled her head languidly to face him, saying "No, not really. If I'm going to participate in both instruction from Lance in the morning and diving with you in the afternoon, I should have an early night."

"Wise girl," he commended, and kissed her gently on her soft mouth.

It was pleasant enough, but with a shock Jill realized it produced none of the sensations in her body Lance's had. And that reminded her of the possibility that he was lying in wait for her back at the house. She didn't think he'd ignore her outright disobedience to his command to stay away from Scott, and that strange tightening sensation in her stomach accompanied her on the ride home.

Scott, perhaps thinking her preoccupation was an aftereffect of the evening with him, remained quiet also as he delivered her back to the Lane house.

He kissed her briefly again at the door, where he left her, as she insisted there was no reason for him to come inside. In actuality, she had no idea what awaited her on the other side of the door and she wanted time alone to fortify herself.

With a brief "See you tomorrow," Scott was gone, the red taillights of his little car diminishing to tiny dots at the end of the long drive before they winked out of sight.

Taking a deep breath, Jill turned to grasp the door handle, and abruptly it was wrenched from her hand as the door was swung open. And there stood Lance, his gray eyes chips of ice in the moonlight.

Chapter Nine

"Come in, Miss Taggert," he said with deceptive calm.

Strengthening her spine and her resolve, Jill stepped across the threshold, then waited while he closed the door softly. She refused to cower, figuring that was exactly what he expected.

"I see you chose to ignore my suggestion about staying away from Dougherty," he observed coolly as he towered beside her.

"It was not a suggestion, Mr. Darrel; it was a royal edict," Jill returned scathingly.

One black brow rose, the firm mouth tightened, and Lance seemed to grow half a foot in height and breadth.

"Oh? Was that how you saw it? I can assure you I have neither the inclination nor the power to order you around. It was merely an attempt to prevent you from embarking on a foolish course. If you choose to disregard the warning, that is your affair."

"I'm glad we understand each other, Mr. Darrel. Now, if you'll excuse me . . . ? I—" She turned to go, but was prevented from taking a step by a tanned hand touching her arm. Startled, she said sharply, "Yes? Was there more?"

Her tone communicated her disinclination to discuss Scott any further, but that wasn't what was on Lance's mind, apparently, for he answered instead, "Yes. Do you have any plans for tomorrow evening?" His expression was guarded, and Jill had no way of knowing what was on his mind.

"Why?" she asked with a combination of curiosity and apprehension."

"I . . . I thought perhaps you would accompany me out to dinner."

Whatever Jill had expected him to say, this wasn't it. If she had been asked to conceive the exact opposite of what she thought would be his likely answer, it might have been this indirect request for her to join him for dinner, and just for one wild moment she wished she could accept. But tomorrow she was diving with Scott, something she didn't want Lance to know.

He moved impatiently, bringing to her attention the fact that she'd been keeping him waiting for her answer. Gathering her composure, and presenting as cool a façade as she could, she refused. "I'm sorry, but I do have plans tomorrow. I—"

"Scott?" Lance clipped out, a frown settling on his dark features.

"I . . . well, yes, we—"

"You don't listen very well, do you?"

Before he could continue his argument against her seeing Scott socially, Jill halted him with some angry words of her own.

"Mr. Darrel, we've already gone over this. You just

admitted you have no desire to order me around, so it seems we have nothing further to say. I appreciate your invitation"—she said the words stiffly, wishing they weren't back to their normal cold war—"but I do have something else going tomorrow. Now, since it's late, and I have a class in the morning, I'll say good night." And turning toward the stairs, she sedately mounted them, all the while feeling his icy regard like a knife in her back.

Once in the safety of her room, she collapsed in a heap on the bed, her legs giving out, her pulses racing. Why did that man have such an awesome effect on her? The thought of continuing their lessons together seemed like some monumental task totally beyond her endurance. But endure it she must, for she was almost through. Her thirty-six hours of instruction were nearing completion. She had already passed some of the written tests, and the end was in sight. For the sake of her beloved uncle, she would do anything, even put up with Lance's chilling disdain.

Undressing quickly and slipping beneath the cool sheet, she determinedly replaced thoughts of Lance with expectation of the dive near the wreck of the 1715 fleet tomorrow, and it was with a satisfied smile curving her lips that she fell asleep.

The following day, after Lance and Jill had completed a morning of written tests, with Jill proving her knowledge of procedure to be excellent, she met Scott in the storeroom, where he was collecting his gear.

"Ready?" he asked, glancing at the tote bag she carried.

"Yes, I guess so. How long will it take to get there?"

"Oh, about an hour. There won't be anyplace to change; got your swimsuit on under that?" He nodded at the jeans and T-shirt she wore.

"Mmmhhhm, and my mask and regulator and fins are in here." She hefted her bag in illustration.

"Good. That's it, then. I'll just put these tanks in the car and we'll go." He led the way out to the parking lot and over to a four-wheel-drive vehicle instead of his little MG. There were already two other men in it. In the back was diving gear and a large duffel bag, a case that looked like an oversized suitcase, plus a small outboard motor. Curious items, Jill thought, as Scott stowed their things alongside the others'.

They got in, exchanged introductions, and were on their way, with Jill sitting in the back beside Scott. The other two—one of whom looked to be in his late thirties and answered to the name of Nick, with the second man considerably younger, closer to Jill's age and named Mike—engaged Scott in discussion of their projected dive, while Jill watched the Florida landscape flow by.

Eventually Scott suggested she eat her packed lunch, since the men had already eaten theirs, which she did.

Due to her excitement, it seemed forever before they were at the location of the wreck. It was a long stretch of golden sand separating palm trees and undergrowth from the surf. It looked wild and untamed, completely uninhabited. The water seemed rougher than the safe little cove, and just for a moment Jill felt her confidence slipping, but a quick look at the three strong-looking men she'd be diving with reassured her.

Nick and Scott were unloading something from the duffel bag while Mike opened the suitcaselike thing, and in a matter of minutes the object was identified as an inflatable boat, complete with wooden floorboards, the small outboard motor mounted at its stern.

When the four of them were suited up with scuba gear in place, they pushed the craft out past the breakers, pulled themselves in, started the motor, and headed for some destination unknown to Jill. She couldn't see how they'd be able to tell one area of the heaving ocean from another, but they seemed to know, for in a little while the motor was cut, an anchor dropped over along with the diver's flag, and all four of them entered the water.

Right at the start, Jill knew the conditions were different. As Scott had said, visibility was minimal, and instead of the beautiful blue, the water was a murky green due to algae stirred up by the vigorous ocean currents.

As they descended, keeping close together, the current would sometimes grab them, as if they were pieces of fluff, and drag them a little way. Swirls of seaweed, bubbles, and dark sand clouds eddied around them, giving Jill the uncomfortable feeling of being encapsulated along with the others in some colossal beaker of sea water, shaken by the fiendish hand of a giant.

The bottom suddenly appeared in sight, and the three men conferred by means of hand signals, then began swimming in the decided direction, with Scott keeping an eye on Jill. Unexpectedly, a large cylindrical object hove into view, and Jill realized with a jolt that it was a cannon, long submerged and now lying in forlorn abandonment. It was impossible to see much more, although they swam around, discovering more cannon, but nothing else.

It was becoming increasingly apparent that the sea was getting restless and treacherous. Jill stuck close by the others, but suddenly a strong current scattered them like a mighty hand dispersing chaff to the wind, and she was lost in an isolated world of green water and sand. Being careful not to panic, she decided the wise course was to ascend, locate the boat, and wait for the others to do the same.

At the surface she saw she was several yards from the light canvas-clad craft, and proceeded to swim for it. It was riding the swells of the restless sea, and with some difficulty Jill managed to pull herself over the low side and to lie panting for breath in the bottom. The ride was extremely unstable, and she wished the others would come quickly. The sky, which had been hazy before, was darkening, the sign a storm was brewing.

Then they were there, all three of them surfacing near the boat, and Jill aided Nick, who in turn helped the others.

"Gosh, it's getting rough," Mike said in exasperation, eyeing the swells of the ocean as if they were his personal enemies.

"Yeah. We'd better head back," Scott said tightly; then: "Are you okay, Jill?"

"Yes," she barely managed to get out. She'd expended so much energy just getting herself to the surface, into the boat, and then helping Nick in that she now slipped into an exhausted silence.

Grim-faced, Nick started the motor and steered the tossing craft back to the beach. No one said so, but they were all eager to regain dry land again. Attempting to dive in the ocean's agitated condition had been a gamble that didn't pay off.

"Now we know why it took them so many years to bring up all that treasure," Mike observed dryly after everything had been replaced in the rear of the Jeep and they were on their way back to Daytona.

"Hmph!" was Nick's only disgruntled response.

Jill, sitting in the back, was nestled into Scott's arms, weakened and bone-weary. Eventually she fell asleep, too tired to remain awake despite the droning conversation of the others as they discussed plans to repeat their attempt to dive in the area that had defeated them.

She didn't wake until they were actually back at the shop and Scott was shaking her shoulder.

"Hey, sleepyhead. Time to get out," he said softly in her ear.

Groggy and disoriented, she didn't become fully aware of her surroundings until an ominously quiet voice spoke from outside the open door. "Dougherty, what in blazes have you been up to now?"

Lance stood beside the car, his jaw square and forbidding, his eyes afire.

Jill jerked to complete consciousness and with a sinking heart slid out of the car. Scott exited after her, his hand comfortingly placed on her waist. Through the lowered veil of her lashes she saw Lance's eyes narrow at the sight of the familiar gesture, then flick to Scott.

"Well?" He directed the terse question to Scott, who stood his ground.

"Nick, Mike, and I went down to explore the site of the 1715 wreck; Jill went along," he explained briefly.

"Did she actually dive in that stuff?" Lance asked incredulously, no doubt familiar with the conditions of the area.

"Yes, but the three of us were there," Scott defended in an angered voice.

"And so you considered it perfectly safe to take along a neophyte like Jill?" Lance challenged, his voice rough with suppressed fury.

Scott's hand dropped from Jill's waist as he straightened in irritation and faced Lance squarely, his hands on his hips.

"Yes, I felt it sufficiently safe for her. As you can see, your pupil survived in one gorgeous piece. Now I'd like to return our gear." With a murderous glint to his eye he stalked past Lance's solid form to join the other two men, who'd been watching this altercation in astonishment, in unloading the jeep.

Reaching out to grasp Jill's arm, Lance looked over his shoulder at Scott and said, "Stow Miss Taggert's gear. I'm taking her home right now," and then he propelled her body, which was too frightened to resist, over to the Mercedes and into the passenger seat.

Wordlessly he started the car and left the parking lot with a roar. Once they were on the highway, he glanced at her pale shaken form.

"For God's sake, why did you allow Dougherty to convince you to go on such a dangerous dive?"

The question proved to be just the goad needed to prod Jill into action. Swinging to face him, she said in a controlled, cool little voice, "Mr. Darrel, just why do you have this penchant for sticking your nose into my affairs? For your information, it was entirely my idea to accompany Scott today." Lance's gray eyes darted to hers, disbelief written in their depths. "He mentioned his plans last night and I practically begged him to take me."

"Why?"

"Because . . . " Jill suddenly stopped, realization hitting her that if she were to reveal to him her desire to discover buried treasure, he would look at it as yet another blackening mark on her character. Too late she remembered how expressive her face was, and before she was able to conceal her thoughts behind a blank facade, Lance looked at her and swore, bringing an embarrassed red to her face.

"So that's it, you little fool. Treasure!" He laughed bitterly. "Did you really think gold was just lying there on the ocean floor waiting for your greedy little hands to snatch it up?

"I should have known it," he continued bitingly. "You're just like that money-hungry stepmother of yours, hoping to get monetary gain by illegal means. I suppose Scott didn't tell you you have to get a salvage permit from the Florida Internal Improvement Fund. And at that, you can't keep all you find."

"Mr. Darrel," Jill interrupted in a loud, angry voice, "it may interest you to know that I am familiar with the Florida Antiquities Act. I am perfectly aware that a salvager must surrender twenty-five percent of all treasure to the state. And as for attempting to get monetary gain by illegal means, that was never my intent. I wanted to repay some of the money Lucy stole from my uncle." Suddenly she clamped her mouth shut. Her true motive had burst out in a flurry of self-defense before she could prevent it.

Mortification compounded horror as Lance threw her a skeptical look, followed by a hate-filled jeering laugh. "Oh, you little devil! You'll have to come up with something more original than that. Either you're a consummate liar or you're more naïve than you look. Do you know the odds against anybody making money hunting treasure?"

Jill lowered her head into her hands, unable to cope with his scorn anymore, and a flood of tears came streaming down her cheeks.

Without a word, Lance tried forcing a handkerchief between her fingers, but she hurled it back at him.

"Oh, just leave me alone! I hate you, Lance Darrel! You're the most hateful man on the face of the earth. You're going to grow into a spiteful, suspicious, lonely old man, and I hope it kills you!" she cried in her pain, then choked in a fit of weeping.

In total silence Lance delivered her to the house. She couldn't look at him, couldn't see if her words had penetrated that ugly thick hide of his. Lunging out of the car, she raced inside and upstairs to her room before anyone saw her. She had to repair the damage to her tearstained face before she allowed her uncle to see her.

In the nurturing environment provided by the lovingly prepared lilac-decorated room, Jill became calm and self-possessed again. That that loathsome man could wield such power to hurt her was becoming evident. She wasn't ready yet to come face to face with the reason behind it. Mechanically she showered, changed into the clingy mauve dress, applied makeup with a heavier hand than usual to cover the ravaged state of her eyes, and then descended the stairs, holding herself regally, like a queen.

Taking a deep, steadying breath, she entered the library. Her uncle was there alone, and an overwhelming wave of relief washed over her.

"Sweetheart, how did it go?" Matt wanted to know as soon as he had delivered a sherry into her hand. Jill had apprised him of her plans to accompany Scott on a dive prior to joining Lance in the car that morning, a morning that now seemed light-years ago.

What she had failed to tell him was where she was going with Scott. Instinctively she knew he might have been restless, knowing where she was, and it had been for the sake of preserving his state of mind, and not interfering with his customary afternoon nap, that she had decided to tell him where they'd gone only after the fact. Not for a moment had she considered this devious. She had been merely looking out for her uncle's welfare.

"Well, we dived in an area unlike the cove," she

began, only to be interrupted by John's tired voice announcing dinner.

"Dinner?" Matt echoed vaguely. "But Lance isn't down yet."

Just then the man in question arrived at the foot of the stairs, changed and looking fresh, his dark hair curling damply over the collar of his shirt. No doubt he'd had a shower, too. I hope it cooled him off! Jill thought sourly.

"Well, if we're all here, I guess we can go on in," Matt suggested uncertainly, looking at Lance. "Did you want a drink, my boy?"

"Yes," Lance said through tight lips, his eyes lingering on Jill's. "I could use one. But you go on in. I'll pour myself one and bring it in." He motioned them on, and Jill accompanied her uncle, her thoughts on the odd look of warning she'd seen in Lance's cold gray eyes.

What was he going to do? she wondered with a growing sense of unease. Make a scene over her alleged dangerous dive? She dearly hoped not. Her uncle didn't need that aggravation. Moving protectively to his side, she gave Matt a brief kiss on the cheek before settling in her chair, which John had drawn out.

"What was that for?" Matt inquired, his affectionate gaze following his niece.

"Just because I love you," she replied easily, as Lance strode into the room bearing a cut-crystal tumbler that looked too generously filled with some amber liquid. His usual Scotch, Jill surmised, watching him settle his long, lean body into the chair at the opposite end from her uncle.

Consuelo came in, depositing steaming bowls of French onion soup in front of them, then retreated to

130

the kitchen to oversee the final touches to the next course.

They began sipping their soup, Lance and Jill less enthusiastically than Matt, until he reopened the discussion they had begun in the library.

"So tell me, where did you and Scott dive today, my dear?"

"Down to the site of the 1715 wreck," Lance supplied suggestively, his eyes watching the older man alertly.

Matt put down his soup spoon with a clatter. "There?" His confused blue gaze fastened on Jill. "But why?"

"Because they're both fools," Lance snapped. "Scott must have completely lost his senses. To take Jill to that area to dive is like throwing a baby into the deep end of the pool. She was in no way ready to cope with that," he concluded firmly.

Jill faced him, her eyes snapping blue sparks. "That analogy is unacceptable to me. You said yesterday I was a good student with the potential to be a good diver."

"Yes, but good, not suicidal! You're not to go diving with Dougherty again! As your instructor—"

"Will you stop this insufferable meddling!" she flared. "I'm sick of it. Every time I turn around, you're there casting a jaundiced eye over my shoulder—"

Lance cut her off with: "That's because I care how your actions reflect on your uncle. Someone has to keep a leash on you—"

"Are you insinuating that I do foolish things, Mr. Darrel? That I don't care about my uncle? May I remind you—"

"The only thing you can remind me of is a—"

"Children!" Matt's bellow cut through the argument like a machete.

Startled gray and blue eyes jerked to stare incredulously at the elder man, who sat tall in his chair, glaring at them. As they watched, the blue eyes gentled, and Matt spoke.

"Now that I have the attention of you hotheaded young folk, I have something to say. And I don't want to hear a word out of either of you until I'm finished." He gave them both disapproving looks, as if they were schoolchildren found fighting in the schoolyard. "It appears to me there has been some kind of contentiousness between you since the day Jill arrived. I had hoped, Lance, that as time went by you would see for yourself what a sweet, genuine young lady she is. And that she is indeed my niece. You, Jill, I had hoped would come to see that Lance's protectiveness of me, born from years of being my only living relative, was not an affront to your character, and that you'd be able to deal with it in time. It seems now that your basic antagonism to each other is born from a fear there isn't room for both of you in my heart." Both Lance and Jill looked shocked, their eyes widening in disbelief, as Matt went on. "You're both familiar with the vastness of the ocean, now. You know there is room there for many living things to live in peaceful coexistence, side by side, benefiting from its life-giving provisions."

He paused momentarily to send them each a penetrating look.

"My love is an ocean," he continued, his voice deepening with emotion. "There is room enough for dozens of Lances and Jills; plenty for only one of each. Both of you mean everything to me. You, Lance, the son I could never have. And you, Jill, the daughter. I love you both, deeply, fathomlessly. Believe that, and try to get along," he implored them, his earnest eyes gazing at them, the love he had for them clearly to be seen.

There was utter silence. Jill felt cut to the heart. Surreptitiously she slid a glance at Lance. He was sitting very still, the anguish written plainly on his face at the pain he had unwittingly inflicted on the man he loved like a father. He was the first to speak.

"I, for my part, am truly sorry for the way my actions have affected you. It is true your niece has stood condemned since she arrived. I will endeavor to give her the benefit of the doubt in the future."

"That's good, my boy," Matt approved with evident relief, then flicked an inquiring glance to Jill.

"I'm sorry, too," she whispered, her head bent. Then she raised pain-clouded eyes to him. "And I'll attempt to get along with Mr. . . . Lance, in the future, also."

"That's all I can ask," her uncle responded, as Consuelo, who must have heard all that was going on, came in with the entrée, now later than usual.

As soon as the plates were set before them, Matt cleared his throat and announced, "Since Jill has been here for over two weeks"—his gaze lingered affectionately on her—"and I hope she stays as long as she wants, even if that means she never leaves . . . I've decided to hold an open house this Saturday night to welcome her. I intend to invite many old friends and neighbors." He stopped to observe the effect this had on the two of them.

Jill leaned forward earnestly. "Uncle Matt, you don't have to do this."

"I know, sweetheart, but I want to," he assured her, his eyes twinkling. "Besides, I've already told Consuelo about it, and she's beside herself with plans. It's been so long since she's been able to flex her culinary muscles, she's flapping like a chicken. But she loves it."

Jill opened her mouth again, intending to reiterate the lack of need for a big party, but Lance stepped into the conversation with words that astounded her.

"That sounds like a fine idea. It's been a long time since you've had a gathering of your friends. It will probably be good for you."

Jill swung rounded eyes to look at him. Had she heard right? If anyone could be expected to object to a gathering, the sole reason for which was to welcome her, it was Lance.

"I'm pleased you feel that way, Lance," Matt was saying. There was more to his statement than was spoken aloud. It was clear he was more than pleased that his adopted son seemed supportive of a plan that, in the past, would have elicited his resistance.

Later, after Jill was in bed, she thought how lucky she was to have such a wonderful, trusting man for her uncle. If only Lance was as trusting. With a sharp stab of pain she realized it meant very much to her to have him change his opinion of her and accept her as Matt's grandniece. This new awareness of her feelings about Lance made her sleep uneasy, and she was so tired in the morning she overslept.

Chapter Ten

Catching sight of the clock beside her bed, Jill let out a wail and bounded out of bed. After hurriedly throwing on jeans and shirt, she clattered down the stairs and went in search of Consuelo, finding her puttering in her kitchen.

"Where's Lance?"

"Oh, Jill! Here, have a cup of nice fresh coffee," Consuelo offered, bustling to the coffeepot to pour Jill a steaming cupful before answering her question. "He's gone on to the shop. He said you need a good day of rest after being so busy yesterday." Her gleaming black eyes assessed the bewildered face of the girl slumping down on the kitchen stool.

Jill rubbed her forehead with one hand while sipping the coffee. "I guess he's right," she admitted reluctantly. "I . . . I slept badly." That was an understatement. In fact, she wished she was back in the bed right then, but since she was already up and dressed, she had to make the best of it.

Thanking Consuelo for the coffee, and refusing breakfast, to the disapproval of the plump cook, Jill wandered in the direction of the office, from where she could hear Matt's voice coming. He was on the phone, and he motioned to her to sit down, which she was only too glad to do. Sinking down in one of the easy chairs, she sipped the remainder of her coffee, her glance running over the wall of books and art objects behind her uncle's desk.

"That's right, Saturday night at eight," Matt said. "You'll be here? Good! I'll see you then."

He hung up, his warm gaze noting the dark circles beneath Jill's eyes.

"Are you feeling all right, sweetheart?"

"Yes, I'm just a little tired." Jill shrugged offhandly, not wanting to have to explain the reason for her restless night to him. "Have you been inviting people for Saturday night?" she asked in an attempt to change the subject.

"That I have, and so far everybody I've spoken to has accepted and is looking forward to meeting my niece," he reported proudly. "What are your plans for the day?"

"Well, I don't know. Lance left without me," she answered a little forlornly.

"I know; we decided it would do you good."

"Oh."

"Consuelo's going into town today to buy all the little extras she says she's going to need for Saturday. Why don't you go in with her and buy yourself a new dress?" Jill opened her mouth to refuse, but Matt cut her off. "Oh, I know. You don't need one. That's just what a girl like you would say, but it's been my experience that

136

all young ladies like new dresses whether they need them or not. I want you to look wonderful Saturday when I present you to all my friends. Now, I want you to go with Consuelo, buy some ravishing creation—go wild—and accept it as a gift from me."

"But, Uncle Matt—"

"Please, Jill?" His kindly blue eyes beseeched her, and she knew to refuse would be to rob him of the pleasure he'd feel seeing her in an outfit provided by him. But how would Lance look at it? Lance be darned! She didn't care; she'd go into town and buy an outfit that would blow his mind.

"All right, Uncle Matt, if it means that much to you," she agreed softly.

"It does, sweetheart. I wish I could make up for all the heartache you've had since your mother died, but I'm afraid it would take more than one dress to do that."

He stood up, holding his hand out to her, and led her into the kitchen to tell Consuelo Jill would be accompanying her. The cook was delighted, especially when Matt laid the command on her to make sure Jill bought the nicest thing they found, regardless of the cost.

Feeling somewhat like Cinderella, Jill drove into Daytona later in Consuelo's car, and before buying the items the cook wanted, some of which would be perishable, they made the rounds of some of the little shops and boutiques. At length, after trying on a dozen or so dresses, they both agreed on one, Jill reluctantly, Consuelo enthusiastically.

It was black velvet, with a multicolored border print, gently shirred at the waist by a gold belt. But the thing that made Jill a little wary, but Consuelo effusively adamant, was that one shoulder was entirely bare, with the other shoulder supporting the front and back bodices by an adjustable tie. One tug, and the top would completely fall away. Jill thought it risqué; Consuelo said, "Stunning." The black dress was bought, boxed, and tucked under Jill's arm before she could think of a good argument against it. She just hoped her uncle would approve.

He did, heartily, later when she modeled it for him.

"Wonderful! Perfect! Consuelo, you are to be commended. One so young shouldn't be so modest about her physical attributes; that's why I sent you along. I knew she'd come back with some gunnysack of a dress."

For the next two days Jill's lessons with Lance were mainly final instructions in open-water conditions. It was more or less a composite of all the techniques she had been learning for the past two and a half weeks. Since they were mostly underwater, Lance could only use hand signals, and when they were through, he retreated to the locker room to change, so their verbal interchanges were brief and related only to diving. Jill was both relieved and disturbed. If this was what Lance had meant by giving her the benefit of the doubt and trying to get along with her, it would never work.

Distractedly she drove herself back to the Lane house on Friday, thinking about Lance's final statement that morning.

"You have only one more session, Miss Taggert, and that will be a comprehensive underwater testing of how well you can perform all of the water work you have learned. Then you will be finished, provided you pass the written test of seventy-five questions."

She'd known the end was coming, but she hadn't expected to experience this strange sense of loss at knowing she and Lance would no longer be together in the mornings. She should be glad—no, ecstatic—she scolded herself, but it did no good.

She parked the car in the garage and walked slowly back to the house, her eyes making a sweep of the comfortable structure. This house had become home to her. She never wanted to leave, and her uncle's words the night he'd announced the party had indicated he didn't want her to leave, either. The only mar on paradise was the tall, dark figure of a distrusting and arrogant man. Were it not for him, the decision would be easy.

Saturday morning dawned in glorious splendor. The sun sent paths of gold across the floor of her room, and birds twittered cheerfully, inviting her to rise and share the beauty with them.

Downstairs, Consuelo was already peremptorily ordering John about as they prepared the house to greet the guests, when Jill padded barefoot and sleepy down the stairs, her nose following the wafting aroma of Consuelo's perfect coffee.

"Ah, Jill! It is your day, eh?" Consuelo chortled from the doorway to the library as Jill paused at the foot of the stairs.

"Come! I'll bring those pretty blue eyes to sparkles when I show you what is in the kitchen."

With a curious and indulgent smile curving her lips, Jill followed the proudly beaming cook out to the kitchen, where she thrust open the doors to the pantry with all the flair of a ringmaster. Jill peeked in, and a gasp of pleasure parted her lips. Consuelo had outdone herself. There on one of the shelves stood a giant cake with a message written across its top: "May my house be yours."

It could be interpreted as an open invitation to all the

guests, but Jill knew it had special significance for her from her uncle. She was overwhelmed, speechless.

"It's beautiful," she murmured, and gave the cook an appreciative hug, which sent the cook back to her work with a satisfied smile splitting her face.

Jill took her coffee out to the porch to drink it slowly; then, when her uncle had failed to put in an appearance, she inquired from Consuelo, who informed her he had gone with Lance to the shop to deal with some sort of business problem.

To fill the void in her day, Jill insisted Consuelo let her help ready the house, overcoming the cook's initial resistance. Finally, when both Matt and Lance arrived for lunch, Jill could ruefully report she had been worked hard, being charged with helping John clear the library of most of its movable furniture, since Matt wanted to provide an area for dancing.

The afternoon was spent keeping her uncle quiet and resting by playing chess with him out on the porch, thereby also keeping out from under Consuelo's busy feet. Lance sequestered himself in the office with invoices and billing. Somehow, Jill felt they were all marking time, a feeling of expectancy hovering over the house.

After eating a very light early dinner, Jill was dispatched by an eager Matt to her room, there to prepare herself for the evening ahead. She treated herself to a long, soaking bath liberally sprinkled with perfumed bath oil and took extra pains with her freshly shampooed hair.

At long last, she was ready, standing before the wicker-framed mirror, casting one last dubious glance over her reflection. The black dress, worn with only earrings—hoops of gold—and a pair of dainty high-heeled black-patent-leather sandals, was stunning. She had to admit that, but there was a wild fluttering in her stomach as she opened her door and prepared to step out into the hall.

Just then, Lance's door opened, and he, too, stepped into the hall, his black brows rising suggestively as those cool eyes made a thorough appraisal of her as she stood poised in the doorway.

"Well, well," he murmured, his voice low and caressing. "So the girl has become a woman."

His eyes dwelt on the creamy skin exposed by the revealing bared shoulder, and she shivered at the seductive quality of his voice and the fire in his eyes.

Well, she'd wanted to cause some sort of reaction in him by her choice of dress, and it appeared she'd succeeded. Perhaps too well.

"He should approve," Lance remarked grimly, and Jill looked at him in confusion.

"Who should?"

"Dougherty! Who else?" was Lance's clipped response before he gestured for her to precede him down the stairs.

She moved stiffly, painfully aware of his roving eye as he followed her down to the living room, where Matt awaited the arrival of his first guests. As she sat beside her uncle, attempting to look unaffected, she was disturbed by the way her bare skin seemed to draw Lance's eyes like a magnet. A disturbing heat spread throughout her body, and she dearly wished she had never succumbed to Consuelo's blandishments to buy such an attention-getting dress.

An inordinate relief came with the sound of the door chimes, announcing the arrival of their first guests. For the next hour people came, crowding the rooms, including Scott and Yvonne. Somehow Jill hadn't given a thought to the secretary's being included, but realized in retrospect the blonde would naturally be invited. She watched Lance offer her a cocktail; then the two drifted off out of her range of vision, and Jill came face to face with the truth that she was jealous.

"Hey, gorgeous, how about a dance?" Scott murmured in her ear, tearing her away from dwelling on this awful realization.

She couldn't be jealous! Because jealousy meant only one thing: that she was, if not in love with Lance, at least attracted to him. That possibility was unacceptable. She refused to consider it. Almost desperately she threw her arms around Scott as he drew her into his arms on the dance floor, and attempted concentrating only on the soft music. There were a number of other couples on the floor, some of which she could remember being introduced to, but none of the names stuck. Only one did—Lance!

"Hey! What's the matter?" Scott questioned, frowning.

Her body had suddenly stiffened as her eyes had seen Lance, with Yvonne held close, dancing in the corner. If what they were doing could be termed dancing, she thought bitterly. They were more like swaying vaguely to the music, and the blatant invitation on the secretary's face would have weakened the resolve of the strongest man. The green bite of jealousy stung Jill into action.

"Nothing, Scott, but I could use one of those drinks John's carting around. Could you snare one for me?" She flashed a brilliant and forced smile at him which sent him off hunting John, while she drifted to the side of the room where her uncle stood with the husband of one of the women who was currently dancing with someone else.

Matt smiled, drawing her into the curve of his arm as he continued the discussion with his guest.

Then, to her horror, the male form that materialized at her side was not Scott, but Lance, quietly asking her for a dance. Darting a quick look at her uncle, she was disturbed to see he had noticed it, and was smiling his encouragement, thereby making it impossible to refuse.

Woodenly she accompanied Lance onto the floor, where he pivoted and swung her into his arms, sending her pulses rocketing and her knees trembling. Oh, please, God, no! Not Lance! she implored silently. Don't let me fall for the last man on earth likely to return my love.

Dreamlike, almost as if she was outside herself, she danced with him, his hand expertly guiding her as they moved as one. The music changed, and still he retained his hold on her, not relinquishing her to any man who attempted to cut in. She felt hot and flustered, especially when Scott returned with two drinks in his hands and watched them on the floor with, first, a perplexed frown, and then speculation.

What could he be thinking? Jill worried, and then all thought of Scott was blotted out by Lance's mouth nearing her ear as he murmured, "Come outside. I have to talk to you." His voice held no cold threat, only entreaty, and Jill, dazed, allowed him to steer her through the crowd, out to the porch, where a soft evening breeze cooled her heated skin.

Holding her hand, Lance led her to a secluded corner of the porch where they would not be instantly seen by anyone entering the porch after them.

He dropped her hand and thrust his hands into his pants pockets, staring wordlessly at her a moment, as she stood, shaking from confusion mingling with anticipation.

"Jill, I . . . " he began with some difficulty, his eyes not quite meeting hers; then abruptly he pulled a sheet of paper from his shirt pocket, handing it to her.

By the dim light of Japanese lanterns, Jill was able to read the paper in her trembling hands, her gentle mouth parting in surprise. Slowly she raised curious eyes to him.

"Why, this is an investigator's report on my father, Lucy, and me."

"Yes," he agreed tersely. "As you can see, it's dated a week ago."

"But . . ."

"And that's not all." He withdrew a second piece of paper, which proved to be a newspaper clipping reporting her father's death and conclusively proving Gordon Taggert died alone. Jill read it absently, having seen it five years before, then handed it, together with the report, back to Lance. His eyes captured hers, and his voice became soft, accented by regret.

"I owe you an apology, Jill. I . . . I judged you wrongly. I'm sorry." The Lance who stood before her now resembled in no way the Lance of the past few weeks. Gone was the suspicion, the caustic manner, and she placed her hand on his arm.

"Thank you, Lance." Her own voice was tight from emotion, and she strove to speak more calmly. "Why did you wait a week to tell me this? Does Uncle Matt know?"

"No, I haven't told him yet." He answered her last question first; then: "I wanted you to know before I told him. And as to why I waited . . . well, I wish I could say I was making absolutely sure you weren't the product of Lucy's warped upbringing, but that would be a lie. One woman couldn't undo at least twelve years of good upbringing. It would be illogical to believe you could be tainted by her greed after the loving mother you had. And she was loving, wasn't she? Matt has told me all about her."

"Yes." Jill's affirmation was feather-soft, memories of her mother filling her heart with pain.

Lance withdrew a second letter from his pocket and handed it to Jill with the words: "This also lent defense in your case. You'll notice Mr. Formby's opinion of you is no less than glowing."

Jill's eyes danced over the print, unable to believe that at last the dark cloud of suspicion that had hung over her for the past weeks was now dissipated by three little pieces of paper.

"But this is dated over a week ago, too. You must have had this for a few days at least." She raised vaguely confused eyes to his, and her voice bordered on being defensive. "You've known I'm not the gold digger you accused me of being for that time, yet you didn't tell me. Why?" Mixed in with the confusion in her tone was pain. How could he have done this hurtful thing?

"Yes." He didn't bother to refute it, which further surprised her. "Remember the night I asked you out to eat?" Jill nodded, bemused. "Well, my plans were to tell you then, but . . . well, as you may recall, you claimed you had a date with Scott." His voice had hardened slightly at the mention of the other man, but then it softened again. "So then, when Matt proposed this party, I felt it would be the perfect occasion to reveal your exoneration. Also . . . " He paused, looking uncomfortable, and she saw his chest rise as he took a deep breath. He was dressed in the same silky patterned shirt he wore her first night there, and she

145

stared at the opening caused by the undone top three buttons where some gold medallion hung on a chain, partially hidden. He rubbed his forehead, and his tone became dry. "You're very young, Jill, not just in age, but in experience. It's obvious in your adult years you've learned nothing about men and how they think. We don't like admitting we're wrong. I'm no different. It took me a while to revise my estimation of you."

"Oh," she said in a very small voice, acutely aware of her ignorance about men and their ways, particularly this man. She looked at him then, and her eyes widened. He was gazing at her, a strange expression in his eyes. But what was astonishing was that his eyes no longer looked like pieces of ice. Why had she ever thought they were flinty and cold? They had the warmth and appeal of fine old pewter, polished with the patina of age.

"Thank you. It means a great deal to me that you told me this yourself. You could have told Uncle Matt first, and left it to him to inform me, but you didn't. Why?"

The intensity of the gray eyes increased, then flickered as he answered: "It seemed the right thing to do at the time. But perhaps it wouldn't have mattered. The end result is the same."

It was an unsatisfying answer, at best, but the expression in his unveiled eyes started a song in her heart. Could it be he did feel for her a measure of what she felt for him? She saw now that her ultrasensitivity to his wounding words had all along been the result of the love growing inside. That was why his icy disdain had hurt so much. She swayed toward him, her eyes searching his, and he grasped her arms in support, drawing her fractionally closer. Hungrily she watched those sensually carved lips move downward, wanting to feel the power of his kiss once more. She closed her eyes and waited.

Instantly she was put from him. Her eyes flew open to see him stepping back into the darkness.

"Save your gratitude for Dougherty; he deserves it," he said icily.

The stinging lash of his tongue dug into her flesh, and with a moan of pain she turned and fled inside through the office. It was dark and no one was there. She fought back the tears of humiliation brought by Lance's cold rejection of her, then, as sedately as possible, went looking for her uncle.

She found him in the dining room, helping himself to some of the delicious hors d'oeuvres Consuelo had provided.

"Uncle Matt?" She regretted the tremor in her voice but was powerless to eradicate it.

"Yes, sweetheart?" He looked up in surprise, viewing her pale face, and concern edged his voice. "Is something wrong, honey?" He reached a steadying hand out to her arm, which was almost her undoing.

Summoning all her self-control, she lied: "I . . . I seem to have developed a headache. It . . . it must be all this excitement. Would you excuse me for a few minutes? I'd like to run upstairs and take some aspirin," she explained calmly, all the while knowi. it was a heartache at the root of her problems, and a whole bottle of aspirin would do nothing to alleviate it.

"Why, of course, Jill, honey. Lie down for a moment, too. Shall I send Consuelo up?"

He looked so upset, she smiled reassuringly. "No, Uncle Matt. I'll be fine. I'll be back before you miss me." And she turned and walked calmly up the stairs, down the hall, into her room, closing the door firmly behind her, and then threw herself on the bed, weeping uncontrollably.

How long she lay there before the door opened, she had no way of knowing. Startled at the shaft of light entering the room, which had been totally dark, she sat up, staring at the silhouette in the doorway.

"Uncle Matt?" she asked tremulously.

The masculine form disappeared as the door was closed softly, and her shocked eyes saw Lance move across the room as surefooted as a cat in the darkness. She flung herself back on the bed, burying her face in the coverlet.

"Go away!" she mumbled, then gasped and swung back to face him as she felt the mattress give. Reaching out in an attempt to push him away, she felt her hands captured by his as he thwarted her efforts.

"Don't be a little fool," he chided softly, but without rancor.

"What do you want?"

"To explain. Now, are you going to stop struggling and listen to me like a good girl?"

She stopped fighting him long enough to snap, "You don't have to explain anything."

"I have to tell you why I refused your very appealing invitation down there. Now, stop it!" He spread her hands over her head, forcing her to lie still, her face inches away from his. He didn't need to say her invitation to what. She was achingly aware he was talking about her desire for his kiss. Her cheeks flaming in the darkness, she subsided, powerless to resist him.

"That's better." He released her arms and sat back. "How old are you?"

"You know perfectly well I'm twenty-two," she retorted.

"How old do you think I am?"

She shrugged, failing to see what his age had to do with anything. "I don't know. Thirty-two? Thirty-three?"

"Thirty-five. Thirteen years older than you, Jill."

"Mr. Darrel, what has that to do with what happened or didn't happen downstairs?"

"I'm too old for you," he stated harshly.

Jill raised her head up to stare incredulously at him. "At thirteen you couldn't even have been my father. What's the point of this?" she demanded. Then she raised herself up on her arms, even though it brought her face much too close to his for comfort, and added, "There isn't an age limit on kissing, you know," in a jeering little voice.

"Jill!" The sound of her name came like a moan of pain. "Do you think it's been easy keeping my hands off you? Refraining from touching you? Like this? And this?" He punctuated his questions by caressing her bare shoulder, then pressing his lips to the pulse beating erratically at the base of her neck.

With a sigh of contentment, Jill wound her arms around his neck and lay back, forcing him to cover her body with his own. Shuddering, unable to control himself any longer, Lance joined his mouth to hers, invading her senses, bringing an ardent response. The pain in her heart receded under the healing balm of his kiss. Mindlessly she moved sinuously against him, instinctively pressing herself closer to his hard length.

She felt a tug at the flimsy tie on her covered shoulder, and then the offending material was brushed aside, yielding place to his warm mouth as he blazed a fiery trail, uninhibited, wherever he dared. His marauding fingers ignited passionate little explosions in their wake, like a ship passing through a mined harbor.

Hotly his mouth settled on hers again, to plunder the sweet treasure she gladly offered, then returned to the much more satisfying task of teasing one breast, until Jill quivered and arched her back, needing something she couldn't quite identify. Deep within her being there was a burning ache, unquenched by the erotic things Lance was doing to her flesh. She thrust her fingers into the crisp black hair and pulled his head up, wanting his mouth to cover hers again. He had no arguments with that, fitting his chisled lips over hers as if they were pieces of a puzzle that needed interlocking.

It was glorious; Jill had never felt this way before in her entire life. Somehow she knew even if one of the boys she'd known back in Kansas had tried to kiss her, it would have been a travesty compared to Lance's expertise.

She moaned, drowning in the mind-blowing experience, totally out of her depth and loving it.

"Oh, Lance," she sighed, her voice quivering and breathless as he removed his mouth to nuzzle her earlobe. "I love you." It came out like a prayer, so deep was her feeling. But its effect on Lance was more as if she'd cursed.

Abruptly he froze, then sat up, rolling off the bed, and she felt it spring back with the removal of his weight.

"Lance?"

"For heaven's sake, cover yourself!" he ground out, raking a hand through his disheveled hair.

Embarrassed and frightened by his sudden change in manner, she pulled the bodice up, attempting to retie it with shaking fingers, which fumbled and failed.

Roughly Lance redid the knot, then retreated to the far side of the room, his face completely in shadows.

"Go back to young Dougherty," he said tiredly.

"You need someone gentle." And before she could think of a reply, he was gone.

But I don't want someone gentle, Jill cried to herself, and a fresh rush of tears forced her to bury her face in the pillow.

Hours later, Consuelo found her, still fully dressed, sound asleep, her head cradled by the dampened pillow. Clucking softly, the cook removed Jill's clothes, covering her with the sheet, and went out of the room, a worried frown on her usually happy face.

Chapter Eleven

The following morning Jill lay in bed, the agony of what had happened the night before working on her like a cancer. To compound it, this was Sunday, and Lance would probably be around all day. How was she ever going to face him? And her uncle? What had he thought when she didn't return to the gathering whose sole reason for existence was to welcome her?

With dread and shame as her escorts, she made her way downstairs. The irrepressible Consuelo was humming in her kitchen, with John astride the kitchen stool morosely drinking his coffee. The lilting Spanish-flavored song stopped as the cook spied Jill hovering uncertainly in the doorway.

"Good morning, little Jill. Your uncle is out on the porch and there is a pot of coffee and a cup for you there, too," she told her, cocking her head to the side to observe Jill with a bright-eyed look.

"Thank you. And . . . and Lance? Is he there?" Jill

just had to ask, not caring what her question revealed about her feelings.

Consuelo snorted and threw her hands in the air in a gesture of disgust. "Ah, he is impossible. A workaholic I call that one. He has gone to that stupid shop to work!" Apparently not seeing the similarity between Lance's working on his day off and herself doing the exact same thing, she continued attacking the glasses and plates piled at the side of the sink, which were leftovers from the evening before.

Partially relieved, Jill forced herself out to the porch. Now to give her uncle some sort of excuse for her disappearance from the party.

He proved to be less of a problem than she'd feared. He accepted her halting explanation of having unintentionally fallen asleep with only the sympathetic comment: "Then perhaps you needed it, honey," and then, his eyes alight with pleasure, he told her about Lance's report, clearing her from blame.

"So, sweetheart, I guess we can get out that bottle of champagne now," he concluded.

Numbly Jill nodded, the anticipation she'd had weeks ago of drinking the toast now destroyed by Lance's ruthless rejection of her love. For what else could it be, she wondered, that caused him to leave her as he had when she'd just been foolish enough to profess it?

Somehow she managed to present a cool, composed countenance at the table later that evening, brightly conversing with her uncle, with only an occasional glance in Lance's direction.

However, after they went to sit on the porch, taking their coffee with them, Matt was called back into the house by a phone call, leaving Jill alone with Lance. She felt as if someone had suddenly stripped her naked and placed her on a busy street for all to stare at. Holding her cup so tightly her knuckles whitened, she pretended to be engrossed with the way the wind moved the branches of the orange trees bordering the long sweep of lawn. So well did she concentrate, Lance's first words caused her to start, almost spilling the coffee.

"Would you prefer Scott to give you your final water-work test and written exam?" His eyes, unreadable pools of silver, seemed to be having difficulty looking at her, but his manner was cool and aloof.

Well, if he could pretend to be unaffected by last night's romantic fiasco, she could do the same. Adopting a casual air, Jill replied, "Why? Don't you have the time for it?"

Her response brought the gray eyes snapping to her in clear focus, causing a shock wave to roll through her system. Why did he look as if *he* was the injured party?

"Of course I have the time," he said levelly, but with just the barest edge to his voice. "I just thought . . . you might be more comfortable continuing with Dougherty. In view of what happened last night . . ."

Jill didn't want to hear him minimize what had happened; she'd never be able to endure the pain. "Nothing happened last night, Mr. Darrel, that could possibly affect our last session tomorrow." Was that cool, unemotional voice hers? How had she been able to achieve it when she was dying, inch by inch, starting with her heart?

A nerve twitched in Lance's firm jaw. "On the contrary; last night proved one thing. You are a young, sexually attractive woman, little more than a girl. You're not aware of your powers to arouse a man, especially one who is used to more than he's likely to get from you." Jill blanched as he continued. "I feel it's best we don't place ourselves in intimate situations—"

"A diving test is hardly an intimate situation," Jill objected, her blue eyes darkened with impotent rage. How thoroughly he was attempting to excise her from his life, like a surgeon cutting out a tumor.

Lance placed his empty cup on a wicker table beside his chair and stood up. His face was now in shadows and unreadable, but there was an odd inflection to his voice as he spoke.

"If that's the way you feel, then we'll conclude your diving exam tomorrow as planned." He took two steps toward the office door, then stopped and added, "However, I think it would be for the best if, after tomorrow, we steer clear of each other." He was facing away from her, his back ramrod straight, and Jill wanted to throw herself at him, holding him close, and beg him not to think like that. But he resembled a granite wall as he stood there waiting her answer: cold, unmovable, and devoid of emotion.

"Yes." Her first attempt at answering was barely a whisper choked by the pain in her heart. She forced volume into her voice, and dredging up the last shred of courage she had, said, "Yes, Mr. Darrel. I think that would suit us both admirably."

Lance's only reply was to step into the darkened office, closing the door behind him. Just for a moment Jill tried convincing herself that the shadows performed by the trickery of the dim light there on the porch hadn't been responsible for the impression she got that Lance's shoulders had sagged suddenly when she answered. But, of course, logic and reason won out, and she knew if he felt anything upon hearing her agreement it was relief and elation.

Her movements jerky, Jill rose and took the discarded china inside and joined her uncle for the remainder of the evening, putting off the time she would have to go to bed. She knew once she was between the cool sheets, her mind would be in a turmoil over what had transpired between herself and Lance, and she dreaded the morning.

When it came, the confines of the Mercedes seemed to have shrunk, and Jill could concentrate on nothing else but the nearness of that masculine thigh, so close to hers. She sat gripping her tote bag as if it was the only thing keeping her from slipping over the brink of sanity. When at last they arrived at the shop, she flung open her door and disappeared into the locker room, mechanically donning her swimming suit.

Lance was already in the supply room, fully clothed in his black diver's suit. He acknowledged her entrance into the room with a lingering glance which ran up her bathing-suited figure almost as if he was powerless to pull his gaze from her. Stiffly she removed her gear from the locker, suited up, and was ready in minutes.

"Let's go," Lance muttered, turning away.

She followed him out to the dock, where they boarded the small motorboat and headed out to sea. Today would be the last of her endurance trials. She would have to perform the rescue technique with Lance, again, followed by an underwater ditch-and-don demonstration. Then she would have to swim underwater twenty-five yards without the benefit of an Aqualung—just holding her breath.

After she had completed all these things, Lance pulled himself into the boat and followed Jill at a slow speed while she swam one-quarter of a mile without stopping. He had measured the distance from a point offshore, almost to the dock, and she swam all the way to the dock, then attempted to pull herself up onto the dock as Lance secured the motorboat to its moorings.

The last thing she wanted was to have personal contact with him, hence her stubborn refusal to allow him to help her up. However, she was more than a little winded from her strenuous testing, and her knee gave out on her as she was trying to gain purchase on the edge of the wet decking, and with a startled cry she fell, knocking her forehead against the dock, then slipped into the water with a moan.

"Jill!" Her name was wrenched from Lance's throat as he watched her sink beneath the waves.

Executing a jackknife dive, his hard lean body cleaved the water, bringing him within a couple of feet of her struggling body. She hadn't been knocked out, only bruised, and now managed to stand up, gasping for air. More than her head hurt; her pride was fractured. The look she subjected Lance to as his tall form came to stand close at her side, a hand on her shoulder providing support, was without warmth and gratitude for his concern.

"Are you all right, Jill?"

"Of course I'm all right," she spat out weakly, as tears threatened to blend with the sea water beaded on her face.

With a muffled oath he gathered her resisting body within his embrace, and no sooner had her trembling feminine contours made contact with his masculine ones than all her resolve never to allow him to touch her again disappeared, to be replaced by the newly awakened longing she experienced in his arms. Fresh tears at her own disability to resist his potent virility began to flow down her cheeks, to be tenderly kissed away by Lance.

Then his mouth found hers, closing over it for a

sweet, drugging kiss. The waves undulated around them, covering them with ceaseless spray. They didn't notice. All they knew was the kiss was unsatisfying at best. As Lance drew her more firmly against his thrusting body, his hands locked behind her hips, fusing them together. The kiss lengthened and deepened until Jill felt she was drowning all over again, only this time in heady sensual delight.

Perhaps, she thought with a wild surge of hope, all his words of the previous evening had been meaningless, backed by some male need to escape forming a serious attachment with a woman.

When he lifted his head, she gazed into his eyes and questioned, "Lance?" in a small aching voice.

The gray eyes became instantly shuttered; the smoldering fires in their depths were extinguished, and he stepped back. Jill felt as if a frigid north wind had suddenly blown between them, freezing her to the marrow. She saw his mouth tilt at an angle she now recognized as a characteristic prelude to some sarcastic remark, and she beat him to it in self-defense.

"Thank you for this last lesson in survival at sea." With that she successfully pulled herself up on the dock, retrieved her gear, and stalked up to the shop without so much as a glance back to see what his reaction was.

As she was wrenching on her dry clothes, there was a knock on the ladies'-room door. It was Lance. Her heart plummeted at the expressionless mask on his face.

"Please complete this written exam," he instructed tersely. "You may do it in the office." Then he was gone, disappearing from her range of vision toward the men's locker room.

Jill finished drying her hair, then gathered up her

things and reluctantly went into the office. Only Yvonne was there, currently talking on the phone, but she must have been informed of Jill's use of the office, for she indicated Lance's cleared desk with a lazy wave of one perfectly manicured hand. Jill sank down on the padded desk chair and lost herself completely in answering the exam. It took her about forty-five minutes, but during that time Lance never returned and the secretary virtually ignored her.

Then, as she was checking her answers a last time, Lance strode into the office. "Finished?" His gray eyes regarded her blankly as she nodded and stood up, handing him the exam. "I'll correct it now and let you know how you did."

"Fine," she agreed stiffly, and left the office to enter the shop. She had no intention of staying around while he corrected her test. Being close to him for any length of time was much more than she could stand.

Scott was in the shop, standing behind the glass-enclosed display case, unlocking it to replace some expensive Aqua-lung regulators he'd been showing a customer.

"Hi, Jill. How'd you do?" He withdrew a box and placed the shiny piece of apparatus in it.

"I don't know. I'm pretty sure I did fine in the open-water part. As for the written exam . . . well, Lance is correcting it now, so I guess I'll know about that shortly."

Scott smiled encouragingly. "I'm positive you've done fine. You're a good diver. If you passed, you should consider trying for an instructor's certificate."

"Well . . . since *you* brought it up," Jill replied in a teasing voice, "I had hoped to take your place when you go."

159

Scott laughed. "I hate to dampen your plans, but you need quite a bit of experience to accomplish that."

"Oh?"

"You should assist an instructor for at least one year, learning, among other things, how to communicate effectively. You should also be able to prove you've been on at least forty open-water dives with at least thirty hours in underwater experience. And after all that, you have to take an instructor-training course, preferably from PADI, the Professional Association of Diving Instructors."

"Oh!" Jill stared at Scott with widened eyes, making him chuckle as he sank down on his haunches to replace the regulator box in the cabinet, thereby taking himself from view.

Just then Lance came out of the office, catching sight of Jill standing in front of the case. He approached, an odd expression on his face.

"Where's Dougherty?" he asked brusquely, and as Jill began to gesture to the unoccupied-looking area behind her, he waved his hand dismissively and said, "Never mind; it doesn't matter." He came to a full stop, inches away. His eyes made a sweep of her body, coming to rest with disturbing intimacy on her slightly parted lips, then her questioning blue eyes. "Here's your test. A perfect score." He handed the exam to Jill, who took it with a startled look at him.

"Perfect?"

"Yes . . . like everything else you do," he muttered, then took a deep breath and looked at her, his eyes hooded beneath slightly lowered brows. "I trust after what just happened out there you can see the wisdom of my proposal last night."

"No!" Jill refuted her previous agreement in a burst of courage.

160

Black brows arched in surprise as gray eyes bore into blue ones. "No?"

Jill looked around wildly, wondering what Scott was making of all this. He hadn't made a move or a sound, and because she was standing between Lance and him, Lance had no idea they were being overheard. Because of that, she could find no words that wouldn't sound like a redeclaration of her feelings for Lance, which she would be embarrassed for Scott to hear.

Lance's hand moved to grasp her shoulder, his eyes once again fascinated by her pink lips, and his head descended just a hair before Jill wrenched from his hold to stand trembling by the huge plate-glass window at the back of the shop.

"I'll not be a handy sex object, Mr. Darrel," she said in a hard voice. "Perhaps you'll find your secretary more accommodating." She was amazed at how icily her words came out, and as she listened, she heard Lance's quick intake of breath, followed by his swift return to the office, slamming the door with a violence that rattled its window.

Her shoulders sagging, she lowered her head and fought to return her pulses to their natural tempo. A pair of hands descended on her shoulders, and she stiffened in shock.

"Relax, honey," Scott murmured. Taking a deep breath, Jill turned to face him, her eyes guarded. "Now I'm beginning to understand a few things," he added speculatively, his mismatched eyes studying hers.

"Such as?"

"Such as why I wasn't qualified to keep you as a student, but I was good enough to teach the general public." He cocked his head to the side consideringly. "A lovers' tiff, perhaps?" A nod of his blond head in the direction of the office showed he was referring to the words that had just been exchanged between Jill and Lance.

"No!" Jill denied too quickly, her cheeks tinged with pink. "We . . . we're not lovers," she continued more calmly. "As a matter of fact, we don't get along at all. Lance can't stand me, and—"

"Okay, honey." Scott's tone mocked her explanation, but he let it stand. "Let me see your perfect test." His request subtly let her know he had heard every word between them, and she handed the test to him with shaking fingers. He examined it, then said, "This confirms my suggestion you aim for your instructor's badge."

"Then do you think you could let me be your assistant?"

"For the three more months I have here; after that, you'll have to team up with someone else." Neither of them mentioned the obvious choice.

"Good. When can we start?" Jill asked eagerly.

"Tomorrow. Help me with my classes in the mornings. And of course, you'll need to start going out on more dives."

"Tomorrow? . . . Er, Scott, could you pick me up and bring me here?" Her eyes had a difficult time meeting his as she phrased this question.

With a quick look at the office door, Scott nodded. "Yes, of course," he assured her quietly; then: "Tell me, are there any objections to you salving your feminine ego by going out with a good-looking man who adores you?" At her surprised and curious look, he bowed. "Said man at your service."

Jill grinned. "No, none at all." And a pain tore through her at the knowledge that what she said was cruelly true. Lance would have no objections whatsoever. He'd probably be relieved that she was spending time with another male, thereby allowing him some breathing space.

"Good. Be ready at six tonight," Scott ordered complacently.

"My, you work fast," Jill teased.

"Have to, baby. I'm only going to be around three more months."

The door to the shop opened, and some customers came in just as Lance stepped out of the office, the keys to the Mercedes in his hand. He gave them to Jill as Scott went to greet the new arrivals.

"Yvonne will bring me home," Lance said tonelessly, and Jill felt slapped.

Without a word, she turned and left the shop, head held high.

Jill began seeing Scott almost nightly. Her uncle approved heartily, despite her arguments that she was spending more time away from him than with him.

"Nonsense, sweetheart," he told her. "It does my old heart good to see you getting about. Where are you going tonight?"

It was a week after she had passed her exam. She had barely seen Lance during the past few days. Frequently, as she and Scott were leaving the drive, Lance would be driving in. She had made it a point to look carefree and gay as his window slid past theirs, but the strain of keeping up such a front was beginning to take its toll on her nerves.

"Oh, I don't know. I never ask. Scott likes to surprise me," she answered now offhandly. She didn't add that she really didn't care where they went, either, as long as it was away from Lance. Scott had taken her to Marine Land and to the Kennedy Space Center. They'd been back to the marina once, this time for dinner, a tender filet mignon that Jill had forced down her tightened throat. That evening had been ruined before it began when she learned Lance was taking Yvonne out also. The only thing that saved it from sheer disaster was that he hadn't taken the blonde to the same place Scott and Jill went to. When they'd returned, the open door of Lance's room showed he was still out, and Jill had tossed and turned, angrily thumping her pillow until she finally heard him return well after two in the morning.

Another week passed, with Scott praising the way Jill was getting on as his assistant. Scott had an irrepressible personality and it made him suggest they go out to celebrate her second week of being, as he put it, "the best helper a diving instructor could ever have." Laughingly, Jill hadn't the heart to refuse him, and when he came to collect her, Matt joined in the gaiety, insisting that Scott join him and Jill for drinks.

Then, as Scott was escorting Jill out the door, his jovial mood prompted him to say, "Don't wait up for us tonight, Matt. The cows will be coming home before us." And laughing, they stepped out the front door.

Jill came to an abrupt halt, causing Scott to collide with her back.

"Hey! What the . . . ?"

The view before them clipped off his words. Lance sat in the Mercedes, but with Yvonne beside him. They were engaged in a passionate embrace, and the memory of what it was like to be on the receiving end of one of his world-shattering kisses made Jill's steps falter, then quicken as she hurriedly made for Scott's car.

Scott followed her more slowly, playfully pounding on the Mercedes' hood, causing the couple inside to break apart in surprise.

Jill's eyes remained glued on the view ahead as Scott joined her in the MG and started down the drive. One piercing look at her pale tight-lipped face, and he realized just what the situation had been all along, but he made no comment.

Taking her back for a third time to the marina, in lieu of his previous choice, he steered her into a quiet, sheltered corner of the antique-decorated bar. Jill was too lost in a pain-filled world of her own to notice the change of plans.

A drink was set before her, bringing her vaguely focused eyes alert and staring at her escort. She saw the look on his face and realized how patently clear her reaction to seeing Yvonne crushed in Lance's arms had been, and lowered her eyes, penitent over her revealing behavior.

"It's Lance, isn't it?" Scott inquired in a voice both oddly soft and harsh at the same time.

Jill nodded, mute before his obvious discomfort.

"Things just aren't going to click between us, are they?"

Shaking her head, Jill whispered, "I'm sorry." And she really was. Loving Scott would be so much easier.

"That's all right," he assured her tightly. "I guess somewhere down deep inside I knew it, but I kept hoping. Sort of like a drowning man hanging on to a raft with a hole in it."

A tear began to roll down her cheek, and before she could wipe it away, Scott had.

"Hey! Don't start that. I can take it. It wouldn't be the first time. It's been my experience, here at least, that once a woman has feasted her eyes on Lance, all other members of the sex seem to pale to insignificance."

"Oh, Scott, what am I going to do?" Jill asked in desperation, throwing a beseeching look with her shimmering eyes.

"Have you tried seducing him?" he asked in a forced attempt at levity.

"Scott," she reproved gently, but his light banter had helped soothe her wounds a little. Then she thought of something, and hunching her shoulders as she sat forward eyeing Scott avidly, she asked, "If you really loved a woman and you had some stupid reason for holding back, what would make you change your mind and go get her?"

Scott looked nonplussed, then answered slowly, "Uh . . . well, I guess seeing her with another guy, somewhat like you seeing Lance with Yvonne tonight."

"Exactly," she replied eagerly. "So I would need to make a rather flamboyant show in front of him—hugging, kissing, and . . . oh, the whole shooting match. Right?" Her eyes were bright with purpose, and Scott looked at her with the beginnings of alarm.

"Yeah, that would do the trick," he answered with difficulty. "Jill, you aren't thinking that you and I . . . ?" he ended lamely, knowing exactly what was going on in her pretty head.

"Yes! Oh, Scott, would you? Please?" she implored him. "Just when he's around. Come to the house at night. We'll sit on the porch practically under his nose and—"

"You don't have to paint me a picture." Scott brought her words to a halt. His mouth twisted in self-mockery. "I should have my head examined, but I'll do it."

"Thank you, Scott. I could kiss you for that," Jill cried in elation.

"Well, that's a start." He returned to his old teasing

self. "Now, have you got your appetite back?" he asked, rising to lead the way into the dining room.

They went home early and sat out on the porch for a while, murmuring softly to each other so anyone in the house would have difficulty deciphering their words. In actuality, Scott was telling Jill about his home state and his plans for opening his own shop. They talked on until a large shape loomed in the door.

"Dougherty, don't you think it's time you were going?" Lance asked levelly.

"Oh? Is it late?" Jill asked casually.

"Very!" was the blunt response.

Scott subjected Lance to the view of an overly long kiss before leaving Jill.

With her eyes demurely cast down, Jill walked past Lance into the house and triumphantly went to her room. If the brooding look in his eyes she'd glimpsed was any indication of his feelings, the staged embrace had done its duty.

During the following week Jill observed Scott teaching his various diving students, including a precocious bunch of small children who reminded her of little tadpoles as they swam in the pool. She helped him out with them, demonstrating her teaching skill to advantage by captivating the little ones.

Once she saw Lance out of the corner of her eye watching her, but she couldn't risk taking her eyes off the busy little bodies to look fully at him.

Every night Scott came to spend time with her on the porch, sometimes joined by Matt, but never by Lance, except when it appeared Scott had overstayed his welcome. Each time he came to hurry Scott on his way, Jill was the recipient of a very passionate kiss from Scott. She was truly sorry Scott failed to kindle an answering response in her. It would have made the way she was using him seem less coldhearted. She feared he still entertained hopes of winning her over, and she was beginning to suffer from the stabs of guilt.

That Sunday, she had actually decided to tell Scott they should discontinue their act, and was sitting on the porch after dinner, awaiting his arrival, when Lance stepped out onto the porch.

"There's a call for you," he said with a jerk of his head toward the study from where he'd just emerged. "It's from lover boy," he jeered as she moved past him into the dimly lit interior.

With a secret smile curving her lips, she curiously lifted the receiver to her ear. "Yes?"

"Jill, Scott here. Listen, I've had bad news from home. My dad has suffered a stroke and I've got to leave right away." He paused to let that sink in. "Tomorrow."

"Oh, Scott! I'm so sorry." Jill was all instant concern, sinking down in the chair behind the desk, which she absently noted was still warm from Lance's occupancy. With a brief look at the door, she saw he had disappeared, leaving her to take the call in privacy. "Is he very bad?"

"They aren't sure, but it looks like he'll have to stop work completely. They . . . they want me to come home and take over." He didn't sound pleased by the prospect, and Jill knew this new development would play havoc with his plans for opening his own shop. "I wanted to call you and tell you I won't be over tonight. I've been packing. I've already spoken to Matt, and he plans to have Lance take over my classes. Do you think you'll be able to assist him?"

"Of course. Don't worry about that, Scott. I know I can manage. Especially with the little tadpoles," she assured him confidently.

"That's my girl. Jill, I . . . I don't want to say good-bye in person. I think you can understand why." His voice sounded grim, and Jill closed her eyes, a pang of sorrow piercing her heart.

"Yes," she managed to get out. "Actually, I think this is for the best. I . . . I was going to tell you tonight that I thought we should cease our charade anyway."

"Yes, well . . . " There was a pregnant pause, followed by: "Then that's it, Jill. Good-bye."

"Yes, good-bye, Scott. And . . . Scott?" She raised her voice anxiously.

"Yes?"

"Write and tell us how things are going, won't you?" Her voice bordered on a plea, and Scott answered a little shortly, "I'll do that," and hung up.

Jill replaced the receiver on the cradle, tears welling up in her eyes for the unnecessary hurt she had caused him. She had learned a painful lesson: Men were not toys you could play with and not expect to break. She covered her face with her hands, then wiped at the tears and stood up, looking straight into Lance's enigmatic face.

He was standing just inside the door, watching her, a tight line to his lips, his hands thrust into his pockets.

"I take it lover boy is leaving you?" he questioned, a harsh accent to his voice.

"Y-yes, tomorrow."

"Did he ask you to come with him?" The glint in his eye was frightening her, and her voice shook slightly as she answered.

"No, he didn't." She began backing toward the door leading to the hallway, her eyes never once leaving Lance's furious-looking face.

"Isn't that exactly what I warned you about? Didn't I tell you he'd leave here a bachelor?" he accused in a blazing voice, and Jill didn't have the courage to tell him why Scott hadn't asked her.

She just stammered, "Y-yes, you did," and turning, fled the room, not knowing Lance misread the anguish on her face.

She located her uncle in the library, comfortably relaxed in a reclining chair, reading a large book with a color photograph of the marine world on its cover.

"Honey, what's wrong?" he asked, catching sight of his niece's disturbed face.

"I just talked to Scott, Uncle Matt."

"Ah, yes. Isn't that a terrible thing about his father? To have a stroke like that and need Scott right away." He patted the hassock beside his chair, and Jill sank down on it, glad to be off her shaking legs.

They discussed the situation for a while, and Jill calmed down enough to ask about the huge photo-filled book he had open on his lap.

"This is a present Lance gave me. See? It's a pictorial dictionary of the coral reefs and all the kinds of life one can find there." He opened the book and began pointing out a number of the wonders of the underwater world. "Look at those huge basket sponges. And this—it's called a gorgonian sea fan. Beautiful, isn't it?"

"Yes, it is," Jill murmured, awed by the delicate lacy fanlike growth, the same beautiful lilac color as her room. "Where can one see things like these around here?"

"You can't. The closest area like this is down in the Florida keys," her uncle explained.

"Oh." Jill sounded disappointed. "That's pretty far for a one-day drive isn't it?"

"Well, you could get there in one day, but there wouldn't be enough time to see very much." Her uncle was looking at her with a speculative gleam in his eye. Closing the book suddenly, he handed it to her. "Here, I've already seen it. Why don't you look at it?"

"Thank you. I will, since it's about as close as I'm likely to get to all this for a while," she responded wistfully.

"Is Lance around?" Matt asked in an abrupt change of subject.

"I think he's in the study."

"Fine." Matt extricated himself from the comfortable confines of the recliner and stood up. "I have to talk to him about something," he said, a strange plotting sound to his voice. "Well, excuse me, my dear?"

"Naturally. I think I'll take this upstairs and soak in the tub before turning in." She stood up, kissed him on the cheek, and followed him out of the room, bidding him good night at the base of the stairs.

The next morning Jill discovered the meaning of her uncle's odd behavior the night before. She had taken her coffee out to join him on the porch and was startled to see Lance there, too, instead of having left already for the shop. Then she realized he'd probably waited for her in view of the fact that Scott would not be picking her up from now on, and she composed herself, sitting beside her uncle.

"Good morning, Jill!" There was a new sound to her uncle's greeting this morning, and a happy twinkle in his eye. "Did you enjoy the book?"

"Yes, I did." She looked hard at him, trying to figure out the cause for his jubilant mood.

"How would you like to see all those things in person?" he asked with barely concealed excitement.

"In person?" Jill cocked her head curiously. "But—"

"Lance and I have been discussing a few things," her

uncle cut her off, able to contain himself no longer. "He is due to take a much-needed vacation, and my business partner in Miami has been nagging me to come down and see some improvements he's made in our hotel. So I've decided we are all three going down there, and Lance has kindly offered to take you diving in the marine sanctuary at the northern tip of Key Largo, called Pennekamp Underwater Park." He made the announcement with great satisfaction that was increased by Jill's stunned, wordless reaction.

Widened blue eyes, crystal clear as the sky overhead, swung to look in astonishment at Lance, who commented softly, "Perhaps that will help ease your wounded little heart."

"Lance," Matt scolded gently but unnecessarily, since Jill didn't have a wounded heart from the source Lance implied.

She swung back to look at Matt. "When are we going?"

"Today," he said. "So run up and pack enough clothes to last several days, young lady," he directed joyfully, and with a squeal of delight, which brought a surprised expression to Lance's face, Jill rose to give her uncle a quick hug before scurrying off to obey him.

Chapter Twelve

Shortly before eleven o'clock they were off in the Mercedes, Matt riding up front with Lance and Jill having the whole of the backseat to herself, along with travel folders, maps, and the big picture book of the coral reef. A beaming Consuelo waved at them, and as Jill watched, John stiffly waved, too. She thought he looked less sullen than usual, and when she remarked about this to Matt, he chuckled and replied, "I think he secretly loves having the house to himself. Consuelo won't be around while we're gone, and sometimes, I expect, her unfailing cheerfulness gets on his nerves.

"Incidentally, I spoke to Yvonne, and she will be canceling Scott's classes until Lance gets back to take them over. It won't be the first time the shop has had to upset its routine."

"Oh," Jill responded, thinking about Scott. She gazed out the window, her brow furrowed, wishing prayerfully he would find someone to love him when he returned home. Somebody was bound to, she reassured herself, and felt relieved of a little of the guilt that had been chipping away at her joyful expectation of diving in the Pennekamp Park.

She had learned their trip would take about five and a half hours, which sounded like an eternity. They would stay the night at Matt's hotel, then tomorrow she and Lance would drive on to Key Largo. The hours wouldn't pass quickly enough, she was sure.

After they had been on the road about an hour, she happened to notice Lance looking at her in the rear-view mirror. Instantly he returned his dark gaze to the road, but she had seen his expression before he looked away, and it perplexed her. It had almost been a frowning, disapproving look. With a flash of insight, she wondered if he was expecting her to be listless and quiet, consumed with grief that Scott was gone out of her life so abruptly. If he expected that, he was in for disappointment. There was only room for excitement over the prospect of diving with him in the wondrous world of corals and fish, and she hummed softly to herself as she turned the pages to the big book. Trying to memorize all the sea life so she'd recognize and be able to identify them if she saw them in the park took all her concentration, and she missed the frequent and fleeting looks Lance threw her from time to time.

After a brief stop at two for a fast lunch, they went on, finally arriving at the tall whitewashed building of Matt's hotel just before six. The sun was still high, but behind the hotel, thus bathing the incredibly white beach in alternate stripes of light and dark as it shone between the side-by-side structures of Miami's hotel row.

They were greeted on arrival by a short, plump,

balding man wearing an outrageously patterned shirt and white Bermuda shorts.

"Matt, you old fox!" he boomed. "What finally brought you out of your comfortable den?" He pumped Matt's hand, his round face shining with the look reserved for old and dear friends.

Matt's expression was a mirror image of it. "Cy, meet my niece Jill Taggert. She's more or less the reason I decided to come down." He drew Jill forward, and she became the recipient of a bone-crushing hug.

"Well!" the man named Cy exclaimed. "I don't know exactly how you accomplished the act, young lady, but I am eternally grateful." He nodded at her uncle and added conspiratorially, "I've been trying to get this wily old coot down here for ages and he always had some flimsy excuse." Then his eyes alighted on Lance. "Lance, my boy! Ye gods! You're down here too? What happened? Daytona blow up?"

Lance stepped forward, shaking his head at Cy's absurdity, and clasped the proffered hand firmly. "I'm taking Miss Taggert down to Pennekamp tomorrow. She's just recently completed a scuba course at the shop and I'm going to reward her efforts."

"Well!" the loud voice responded, and Jill wondered if Cy ever talked at normal decibels. "This calls for a celebration! Matt, you have your usual suite. I've put Lance and Miss Taggert next door. Not together, though," he added mischievously as Jill's cheeks flamed out of control. He swung to snare a bellhop. "Bobby, take these people's things up to the Presidential Suite," he ordered in a voice that wasn't condescending, but friendly, and Jill's heart immediately warmed to him. It was what one would expect: Matt Lane would never be in business with some hard-nosed, money-first/people-second individual.

175

Bobby led them to the elevators, which took them to the top floor, and saw their luggage was deposited in the correct rooms. Matt came to see if her room next to his, was all right.

"Uncle Matt, I don't need a room this large," she protested as her wide blue eyes surveyed the beautifully appointed room with its king-size bed.

"Nonsense. When you deserve to be treated like royalty, accept it." He offered her his arm in a courtly manner. "Shall we go down to partake of the feast Cy has no doubt spread out for us?"

Cy's spread resembled the medieval groaning board. In a private salon off the main dining room, he had had a table spread with a smorgasbord the likes of which Jill had never seen. Buckets of shrimp, with bowls of cocktail sauce on the side, were followed by salads and hot dishes, ending with a huge slab of roast beef kept warm by a heat lamp. Jill's eyes widened at the near-ostentatious treatment Cy gave Matt, but she realized Cy probably did everything in a big way, making him the logical one to actually be on the scene at the hotel.

Various employees made time in their busy schedules during the evening to slip in and express their obvious pleasure at Matt's visit. Jill sat beside Lance, observing her uncle talking animatedly to an older employee, and then Lance leaned over to whisper in her ear.

"With treatment like this, one wonders why he comes down here so seldom." His warm breath fanned her cheek and disturbed the rhythm of her heart.

She tipped her head toward him, getting a whiff of his after-shave, and her voice faltered a little. "Y-yes. I guess that's just one facet of his personality: a shying-away from the limelight."

With difficulty she raised her eyes and looked straight

into his, and her breath became trapped in her chest. There was such a smoldering sensuality about his expression, she felt mesmerized.

"Jill, I—"

Whatever he was about to say remained unstated as Cy loomed over them, jovially exploding their quiet little world. "Lance! Come back to the kitchen with me. I want to show you that new system I devised for dealing with incoming orders."

With a wry grimace and an apologetic shrug, Lance left her, following the portly figure of the talkative Cy.

Jill smiled as she watched him, understanding one reason, perhaps, why Matt didn't frequent the hotel more often. Cy could be a bit overbearing.

Later, after Matt had visited with the majority of the staff, who, Jill suspected, found his quieter temperament pleasing after being exposed so much to their resident boss's, the three of them repaired to Matt's suite to have a nightcap.

Cy joined them, his irrepressible chatter making any renewal of the aborted conversation between herself and Lance impossible.

At one point Cy asked Matt why he wasn't going to dive Pennekamp with Jill and Lance, and her uncle replied, "I want Jill to have only diving on her mind tomorrow. You know, since my attack I need another male diver there besides Lance."

"What happened to that other boy you have working for you?"

"He left this morning. A family problem at home caused him to have to leave us almost three months ahead of time," Matt explained sorrowfully.

Jill felt gray eyes burning into her, and she slid a glance at their owner, which revealed he was watching her closely. Did he expect some outward sign of grief over Scott's early exit? Meeting his look unblinkingly over the rim of her glass, she sipped the sweet mixture contemplatively. Why did Lance seem so preoccupied with her emotional state over Scott's departure? Or was she reading more into his searching looks than was warranted? It irritated her that she knew so little about men and how they thought. Without Scott there to advise her, she hadn't a clue how to proceed in her attempt to attract Lance. She'd never tried getting a boy before, let alone a man. She felt totally out of her league dealing with this confounding man. Shelving the problem, she returned her attention to the conversation between Matt and his business partner until it was time to retire.

The following morning, Lance and Jill started out on the hour's ride to Key Largo with Matt's exuberant blessing. He stood beside Cy, who was eager to show him the recently refurbished hotel, watching them until they were out of sight.

The previous night there had been a subtle change in Lance's manner toward Jill, and she sat beside him in the Mercedes, her pulses behaving like a seesaw.

He drove with the assurance born of familiarity, taking U.S. 1 across the bridge onto the upper keys. Key Largo resembled the more densely populated area around Miami, whereas the lower keys were where one could find the tropical-island-like areas. But they weren't land tourists; they were bound for the world beneath the waves.

Renting a boat, complete with a salty old skipper looking like he'd just stepped out of *Moby Dick*, they headed out to sea. For their dive, Lance had said they needed to wear only the short-sleeved half-suits, although he'd insisted they needed gloves to protect them from the sometimes treacherously sharp coral. As the boat cut through the water out toward Pennekamp, they put on their gear.

Jill zipped on her suit; then her hand paused as her eyes fastened on the sight of Lance's almost naked body. The thin covering of the full neoprene had never even hinted at what a powerful build he had. Rippling chest and bulging arm muscles pulled the half-suit over his tall, tanned frame as Jill tried uselessly to drag her gaze from the disturbing sight. His overpowering masculinity made her wonder whatever had possessed her to set her sights on him. She couldn't have been thinking straight to imagine he cared for her. Despair over her incredible naiveté forced her back to the act of donning the remainder of the scuba gear. She strapped on her fins as the skipper cut the engine and informed them they had arrived at their destination.

Lance preceded her into the water, waited until she was beside him, and then gave the thumbs-down sign for descent. They were diving fairly shallow, only around twenty to twenty-five feet, because Lance said that was where the most color was. And indeed, there was, Jill noted with a feeling of wonder never before experienced. As they neared the bottom the blurred tapestry of color clarified into recognizable patterns.

With undiluted joy, Jill swam along, able to see the reality of the things she'd seen in the book. Huge brain coral, elkhorn and staghorn coral, the beauty of the filigreed sea fans, all vied for her attention. But what impressed her most was the vast numbers of fish life. They hung like clouds, assessing Jill as unashamedly as she did them. Sometimes it was almost impossible to see around her as the mass of shining bodies schooled past. She reached out and felt them slide past her arm, unalarmed. This blasé unconcern must be due to the frequency with which divers swam in the area.

Jill didn't even bother to swim after a while; all she had to do was hover at the bottom watching the constantly changing kaleidoscope of life swarm by. There were the yellow-and-white porkfish with their vertical black stripes, the silvery fish she recognized now as grunts, and the beautiful blue-green angelfish.

Her mind couldn't take it all in. She looked for Lance and found him only a few feet away, observing her as intently as she had been watching the fish. The polished pewter of his eyes sent shivers through her body, and then her attention was snatched from this disturbing fact by jellyfish, the size of dinner plates, pumping past.

In the awesome silence, broken only by the sound of her own breathing, she felt like a sinner on sacred ground. For thirty more minutes, until their air supply ran low, they glided gracefully along, examining this underwater temple to divine creativity. Feather-duster worms, coral-colored spirals of spiky protuberances, adorned growths of star coral. Giant sea whips, resembling fuzzy green cacti, reached their arms toward the light in a silent kind of worship.

When at last Lance signaled their time was up, Jill felt an incredible sense of loss. It was as if there would be no slaking her thirst for this underwater splendor. She knew there would never be enough times for her to visit the reef and be satisfied.

They broke the surface beside the boat, and the grizzled skipper helped Jill mount the ladder. Lance followed her in, and as she removed her tanks and regulator, she couldn't contain her enthusiasm.

"Oh, Lance!" she cried. "It was wonderful! Words can't express adequately how incredibly beautiful it all was. Thank you so much!" Her eyes locked with his, and it was as if some supercharged emotions sparked an arc between them coupling their hearts, and she felt shocked to the core with the depth of feeling she saw in his eyes.

She opened her mouth to speak and was cut off by the skipper saying, "You two folks ready to return to port?"

"Yes," Lance said without breaking that intangible link between himself and Jill to look at the skipper.

The launch started up and headed into the westering sun. It was a little past noon, but already the sun was dipping down, following its inexorable path to earth. Jill shielded her eyes from its glare and collapsed on the padded bench at the back of the boat. The smell of salt water combined with mildew wafted to her nose and she wrinkled it in vague distaste. Lance sank down beside her, the sound from the inboard motor making conversation out of the question.

He groped for her hand and held it in his warm grasp all the way back to the dock. Jill was too stunned and happy to remove it.

At the dock, the skipper cheerfully offered to take them out again anytime, then wandered off to his little dockside shack.

Lance stowed their tanks, regulators, and fins in the trunk of the Mercedes, then began unzipping his half wet suit. Jill followed his example, slipping out of the dark blue top and laying it on some towels; then she noticed something odd about his behavior. Turning her head, she saw he had unzipped his suit only partway and had stopped, and was now regarding her with a curious expression.

"Even with your hair plastered wet around your ears, you're beautiful," he muttered thickly.

Jill caught her breath, eyes wide, her mouth parted in unconscious invitation to be kissed. With a muffled groan, Lance succumbed to the silent appeal, cupping her face with his big hands and crushing her mouth under his. Her lips were ground against her teeth and she almost felt as if she was being punished for some flagrant wrong she was ignorant of having committed. Try as she might, she couldn't think of a reason.

Suddenly the pressure decreased and became sensual and coaxing. Then Lance dragged his mouth from hers to murmur hoarsely in her ear. "Answer me one thing," he demanded.

"Yes?" Anything; she didn't care. She just wanted to savor the taste of his lips again, not talk.

"Did I get my signals crossed? Or is it true Dougherty means nothing to you?" His deep voice almost had a desperate quality to it, and she raised disbelieving eyes to stare at him.

"Dougherty who?" she replied impishly, and was rewarded with a brief but fierce kiss.

"Do you have any idea of what you've put me through these past couple of weeks?" he questioned gruffly.

"How?" She eyed him innocently, and his arms tightened around her almost unbearably.

"As if you didn't know," he growled. "Sitting with him oh so cozily on the porch each night. Every time I turned around, you were together. Teaching, diving, going off in that ridiculous little green car of his. I could beat you unmercifully for that."

She quivered with pleasure at the passionate ring of possession in his voice, snuggling closer to his strong wide chest, her nose tickled by the cloud of hair revealed by the half-open zipper.

"There is one thing, though . . . " He paused and placed his hands on her shoulders, forcing her to back up.

She looked into his troubled eyes. "What?" She

wasn't interested in continuing the discussion, and her gaze fastened on his well-shaped mouth, yearning to feel its pressure on hers.

He shook her gently, snapping her attention to his wary eyes.

"Why were you crying after you talked with Dougherty Sunday night?" There was so much pain in his voice, Jill hurried to explain it away.

"Because I had used him so shamefully."

"For what?"

"I wanted to . . . " She stopped, a becoming flush flooding her cheeks.

"Yes?" Lance looked about at the end of his tether, and his hands curled painfully into her slender shoulders.

"I wanted to make you jealous!" she stated baldly, eyeing him alertly to observe the reaction this remark produced.

"You what? Why, you little . . . " He bit off what he was about to say and hauled her into his arms, his kiss a mixture of pain and pleasure. "Well, it worked. I was out of my mind, eaten up with love and having to watch you two together. And all the while it was just an act!" He laughed softly, a rueful tilt to his mouth. "Oh, I can see I underestimated you, you little devil. You're no girl. You're a full-grown woman."

"And I'm all yours," Jill sighed, melting against him.

"Then you'll accept this?" he questioned, reaching inside his wet suit. His gray eyes searched hers, sending some message she couldn't fathom. "I seem to have brought something up from the bottom," Lance commented with an enigmatic voice.

"What?" Jill strained to see inside the suit, but all she could see was his chest, with its liberal covering of hair, and her pulses soared.

"A piece of treasure. I hope you like it."

"Treasure!" She laughed incredulously. "That's preposterous."

"Nonetheless, this is what I have," he insisted in a vibrant deep voice, and pulled a small glittering object from inside his suit.

Jill's soft mouth parted, but no sound came out as she glimpsed the shining diamond ring he held, its brilliance reflecting the sun's glory in a many-faceted rainbow.

"But you can't have found this in the ocean," Jill objected, bewildered. "In the first place, it's not all black from the salt water."

"Oh, but I did." Lance's handsome mouth formed a wide smile. Reaching out for her left hand, he said, "I found it in that ocean of love Matt talked about."

Shimmering blue eyes spilled over with joyful tears as Jill threw herself unabashedly at Lance.

"Then you do really care for me!" she crowed, and was immediately subjected to a crushing embrace as Lance parted her lips with his in a devastating kiss, unmindful of any passersby in the parking lot.

"And, yes, I do accept it," she softly answered his earlier question, and spread her left hand expectantly.

Lance's fingers suddenly closed over the ring, hiding it from view. "Well, you can't have it."

"What?" Troubled blue eyes searched shuttered gray ones.

"Until I hear you say you love me," he explained, looking aloof and withdrawn, as if he had doubts she would.

"But I did, the night of Uncle Matt's party."

"Yes, but I want to hear you say it in the cold light of day, not after I've been making love to you."

"Oh," Jill murmured, eyes downcast to hide the

teasing lights in their depths. "I love you, Lance Darrel," she obliged simply, and raised brilliant blue eyes, all the love she felt for him there for him to see, and the ring was placed on her finger before Lance kissed her in a thoroughly satisfactory manner.

After a very long time, Lance reluctantly pulled his lips from hers.

"When did you first fall in love with me?" Jill asked, her love-soft eyes gazing at him as if she worshiped the shape of his face.

Lance chuckled ruefully. "Probably from the first moment I saw you standing so forlornly in the midst of the airport. You were so exactly the opposite of what I expected. I was looking for some worldly, calculating-looking woman, the type that would bring nothing but trouble to Matt, so when I saw this sweet, defenseless little kid, I couldn't reconcile it. I decided it had to be a cleverly devised front."

"Ah," she murmured, then looked at him, a faintly jealous glint in her eye. "I was expecting Yvonne then, not a man. And that brings up a question of my own about past love affairs."

"Yes?" Lance's mouth tilted as if he knew what she was about to ask, and her heart tilted at an identical angle at the sight. He was so good-looking, it made her body react crazily. But she wanted something straightened out, and got her erratic pulses under control again.

"I'd like to know about her. Just what *was* the relationship between you two?" Her tone had become faintly apprehensive; she almost didn't want to know. Perhaps they had been lovers until just a few weeks ago, and the possibility filled her with revulsion.

"There wasn't any." His first words shocked her so much her mouth dropped open in disbelief.

"None?" she almost shrieked.

"None." Lance shrugged carelessly. "Not that she didn't make it perfectly clear that, given half a chance, she'd grab it. But her husband was my friend. He was also one of our scuba instructors. He died two years ago in an accident."

"Diving?"

"No. That would have been the greatest irony. Actually, he was killed in an automobile crash." This revelation caused Jill to wince, and Lance crushed her in his comforting embrace. "I know," he said into her hair. "A lot of people get killed in car accidents every year." After a quick kiss on her temple, he continued. "Hugh, Yvonne's husband, was one of the best friends I ever had, and when he married her, I thought he was making a big mistake. She's the type to marry a man for what he can give her, not for love. He was blinded by her beauty, and after only one year of marriage I could see things were going sour with them. That's when she began making subtle plays for me. I tried to tell Hugh, and we had an argument. He went out and drank too much, went home to confront her, and they had some terrible argument, too. He left the house, never to come home again. That night he ran his car into an embankment, and—" He was silenced by the tip of Jill's finger laid across his lips.

"That's all right. You don't have to tell me about it." She hurt for him, for the pain she had caused by making him recount an incident that so obviously still caused mental anguish. He kissed the finger, then went on.

"After his death, Matt hired her as secretary. I always said Matt couldn't resist a pretty face and a sorrowful story, but as it turned out, in this case she did earn her keep. She really is one darn good secretary. But I think she thought by working at the shop she'd be able to get me to succumb to her charms easier if I was near her all day. I've managed to resist her for the most part."

"Wait just a darn minute. I wouldn't call the way you were kissing her that night you brought her home with you, when Scott and I were going out to dinner, exactly ignoring her or resisting her." Her eyes flashed blue sparks as she remembered the way she'd behaved with Scott that night after seeing that display.

"Correction. She was kissing me. And let's face it, I'm a man, with a man's tendencies." Again that careless shrug. "Besides, I was denying myself your company, so you can't blame me for allowing her to do it." His eyes teased hers, but she looked disgusted.

"Well, I expect complete fidelity from now on, Mr. Lance Darrel."

"Yes, future Mrs. Lance Darrel. Were you jealous?" The warm pewter eyes crinkled as he questioned her.

"Yes," she almost hissed, then laughed.

"Well, then you can understand how I felt about all the time you were spending with Scott. When I first saw you at the airport, I didn't know I loved you then, but that first day I took you to the shop and you and Dougherty seemed to get on together so well, I was beginning to experience those irksome twinges. I tried telling myself I was angry that your sweet, innocent looks had hoodwinked him into trusting you, just like I thought they had Matt. But eventually I had to come to grips with the truth. You had my pelt to add to your collection." His words held no bitterness, and neither was there any regret in the glittering look he gave her as he added, "Matt will be pleased."

"Yes." She didn't need to say any more. They both knew Matt's happiness would know no bounds when they told him the news.

"Let's go tell him that together we've found an ocean of love all our very own," Jill suggested, her eyes dwelling on the man she adored.

Lance guided her into the passenger seat, closed the door, then leaned in through the window to kiss her flushed cheek. Before getting in and heading the Mercedes north, he added fervently, "And I hope we drown in it!"

Silhouette Romance

IT'S YOUR OWN SPECIAL TIME

Contemporary romances for today's women.
Each month, six very special love stories will be yours
from SILHOUETTE. Look for them wherever books are sold
or order now from the coupon below.

$1.50 each

Hampson	☐ 1 ☐ 4 ☐ 16 ☐ 27 ☐ 28 ☐ 40 ☐ 52 ☐ 64 ☐ 94	Browning	☐ 12 ☐ 38 ☐ 53 ☐ 73 ☐ 93
Stanford	☐ 6 ☐ 25 ☐ 35 ☐ 46 ☐ 58 ☐ 88	Michaels	☐ 15 ☐ 32 ☐ 61 ☐ 87
		John	☐ 17 ☐ 34 ☐ 57 ☐ 85
Hastings	☐ 13 ☐ 26 ☐ 44 ☐ 67	Beckman	☐ 8 ☐ 37 ☐ 54 ☐ 72 ☐ 96
Vitek	☐ 33 ☐ 47 ☐ 66 ☐ 84		

$1.50 each

☐ 5 Goforth	☐ 29 Wildman	☐ 56 Trent	☐ 79 Halldorson
☐ 7 Lewis	☐ 30 Dixon	☐ 59 Vernon	☐ 80 Stephens
☐ 9 Wilson	☐ 31 Halldorson	☐ 60 Hill	☐ 81 Roberts
☐ 10 Caine	☐ 36 McKay	☐ 62 Hallston	☐ 82 Dailey
☐ 11 Vernon	☐ 39 Sinclair	☐ 63 Brent	☐ 83 Halston
☐ 14 Oliver	☐ 41 Owen	☐ 69 St. George	☐ 86 Adams
☐ 19 Thornton	☐ 42 Powers	☐ 70 Afton Bonds	☐ 89 James
☐ 20 Fulford	☐ 43 Robb	☐ 71 Ripy	☐ 90 Major
☐ 21 Richards	☐ 45 Carroll	☐ 74 Trent	☐ 92 McKay
☐ 22 Stephens	☐ 48 Wildman	☐ 75 Carroll	☐ 95 Wisdom
☐ 23 Edwards	☐ 49 Wisdom	☐ 76 Hardy	☐ 97 Clay
☐ 24 Healy	☐ 50 Scott	☐ 77 Cork	☐ 98 St. George
	☐ 55 Ladame	☐ 78 Oliver	☐ 99 Camp

$1.75 each

☐ 100 Stanford	☐ 105 Eden	☐ 110 Trent	☐ 115 John
☐ 101 Hardy	☐ 106 Dailey	☐ 111 South	☐ 116 Lindley
☐ 102 Hastings	☐ 107 Bright	☐ 112 Stanford	☐ 117 Scott
☐ 103 Cork	☐ 108 Hampson	☐ 113 Browning	☐ 118 Dailey
☐ 104 Vitek	☐ 109 Vernon	☐ 114 Michaels	☐ 119 Hampson